# Point of Order, Mr. Chairman

*Ted Sherrell*

To Nancy,
A Lady Whose Charm, Integrity, Intelligence and Personality Ensures That She Is Not Included Amongst the Very Peculiar People Who Are To Be Found Within the Pages of This Book. Best Wishes, Ted Sherrell

# Point of Order, Mr. Chairman

by

*Ted Sherrell*

Adelphi Press
4 - 6, Effie Road, London SW6 1TD

Copyright © 1993 Ted Sherrell

Printed and bound in UK
Published by Adelphi Press
ISBN 1 85654 098 7

# Contents

|  | page |
|---|---|
| *Chapter One:* The Flagpole | 1 |
| *Chapter Two:* The Chapel of Rest | 37 |
| *Chapter Three:* The Twinning | 73 |
| *Chapter Four:* The Tree | 93 |
| *Chapter Five:* The Curtains | 109 |
| *Chapter Six:* The Bridge | 127 |
| *Chapter Seven:* The Emergency Committee | 141 |

# THE FLAGPOLE

Frank Jackson glanced, covertly, at his watch. Twenty to ten - and there was football on television at ten o'clock. It was certainly dragging on tonight. The longest meeting for months, in fact. It was Mrs Gilbert's fault as usual. Trees - that was all the woman thought about. She had been on the council six or seven years and he'd never heard her talk about anything else.

And she had to choose tonight, when there was already a long agenda, to read out a list of fifty different trees and shrubs, she thought the council ought to buy, to plant in the park. All in Latin, too. Nobody had ever heard of any of them. And who cared anyway. Like Arthur Phillips said, half of them would be ripped up within a week, and the rest would die of root rot with all the rain they had. But nothing would stop her reading out her infernal list and now here they were at least half an hour later than they need have been - and the Cup replay less than twenty minutes away.

And Cecil Conway didn't help. He'd take a thousand words - and half an hour - to say good morning, would Cecil. Quite a competent town clerk in his way, but he could always bring complications to the simplest problem. And time; like just about everybody connected with this council, he was a master at wasting time.

"So that's the gist of the letter, Mr Mayor," droned the town clerk, referring to a communication from the town Civic Society.

"It would have been a damned sight quicker if he'd read it out," muttered Councillor Tom Gaskell, his mind, likewise, upon the fast approaching Cup replay. "So what's new?" retorted

1

Councillor Jim Sparks, sitting beside him. He moved upwards slightly from his half reclining position, raised his voice slightly, and gazed at the Mayor.

"Move no action, Mr Mayor," he said.

"Thank you, Mr Sparks," replied Frank Jackson. "Do I have a seconder?"

"Can I hang a hat on this one, Mr Mayor?" Councillor Mrs Beckett hauled her considerable bulk to its feet. "You see, whilst I agree we should take no action on this letter, I do feel that there are one or two points raised....."

"Do I understand you're seconding Councillor Sparks proposition, Mrs Beckett?" interjected the Mayor.

"Well, yes, in a way but....."

"Thank you, Mrs Beckett. The motion's been proposed and seconded - all in favour."

There was a communal grunt, a few arms moved in desultory fashion - and Town Mayor Jackson smiled happily. "Thank you, ladies and gentlemen - the motion's carried." "Now if there is no other business, I declare the meeting....."

"Hang on, Mr Mayor," cried Douglas Denny, clambering noisily to his feet. "I'd like to ask the town clerk why the Union Jack on the town hall tower was flying at half mast yesterday on the occasion of the Queen's birthday?"

"I've had no notice of this question, Mr Denny," rasped the Mayor fiercely. "You've been on this council long enough to know that it's customary to give me notice of anything you wish to bring up under 'any other business'."

"I appreciate that, Mr Mayor - and I apologise. But I've been unable to contact you. I did phone your home at lunchtime but your wife told me that you've been away on business for a couple of days and wouldn't be home until early this evening -

just in time to attend this meeting."

"Yes - yes, well that's quite true. Anyway, what's all this about flags at half mast?"

"It's obvious you've been away, Mr Mayor, else I reckon you'd have heard about it, all right. In fact I've been pestered all day about it - people stopping me in the streets, telephoning me at home and so on. I reckon you must have had numerous complaints here in the office," said Denny, looking at the town clerk.

"Well - yes. There have been a few ratepayers making comment about it," replied Cecil Conway. "It's the sort of silly little thing which people tend to get worked up about."

"Silly little thing, be damned!" roared Denny. "Mr Mayor, I don't call a deliberate insult to Her Majesty the Queen a 'silly little thing'."

"Or to the Mayor of Pontville, Sur La Mer," interjected Councillor Nigel Hollins, Chairman of the Twinning Committee. "It almost caused an embarrassing incident when the French party were here last week."

"In what way, Mr Hollins?" asked Frank Jackson, a further furtive glance at his watch causing him to write off the first half of the match.

"Well, Monsieur Mallion, the Mayor, looked up at the tower as the town band was playing the French National Anthem, saw the Tricolour at half mast and thought we were deliberately insulting him - and France. It took a bottle and a half of Scotch to convince him that obviously the wind, or something, had made it slide down the flagpole." He glanced malevolently at Conway. "I complained forcibly to the town clerk and he told me he would look into what had happened. I might have saved my breath by the look of it. The fact is, Mr Mayor, we pay our officers very generous salaries, and have a right to expect a little efficiency in return."

Cecil Conway jumped to his feet, his glasses almost falling off in the process. "Mr Mayor, I must protest at Councillor Hollins' grossly unfair attack. I would remind him - and everybody else on the council - that my salary is far lower than many other town clerks serving towns no larger than this one. Also, a couple of years ago, you will remember that I volunteered to forego my annual increment to help the town's finances after the extra expenditure we incurred when we had to replace the town hall floor because of dry rot."

"And whose fault was it we didn't have enough money to do the job properly?" retorted Hollins. "If the town clerk had put a sensible amount in the estimates to do the job then the crisis would never have happened. £1,000 he put by, Mr Mayor, and in the end it cost £12,000. If I ran my business......"

"Mr Hollins, please - that's enough," snapped the Mayor, his gavel having a rare outing as it thundered against the polished block of wood provided. "We're in open council at present. This sort of thing should be discussed in committee. Not that we're going to go into committee," he added quickly. "The town hall floor is an issue over and done with......."

"Thank God," muttered Councillor Mrs Crosby.

"...... and I see no need to resurrect it. The questions at the moment would appear to be, why are the flags being flown at half mast, and what are we going to do about it?"

"Perhaps I can help, Mr Mayor," said Conway, his composure regained. "We have had a few problems with the flagpole on top of the Town Hall tower. I know that the Works Supervisor tried to put the matter right twice last week when the Tricolour wouldn't go any further than halfway up the flagpole, but he's had a number of other problems to deal with, and hasn't been able to give the matter his full attention."

"I don't care what his other problems are - sorting out that flagpole would appear to be a priority," said Hollins. "After all, we can't go upsetting folk the way we are at present. But then, Mr Mayor, the works supervisor should be here in person to tell us what the problems are and why he hasn't solved them. Where is he?"

"I'm afraid he's off sick, Mr Mayor," said Conway. "A nasty bout of the 'flu."

"That's a pity - but I know there's a fair bit of it about," replied the Mayor, wearily. "Obviously we can't really discuss this without the works supervisor being present, so I would suggest it be put on the agenda of the next Properties Committee meeting, when, hopefully, Mr Benson will be over his 'flu and can tell us exactly what the problems are regarding the flagpole."

"Well, - er, unfortunately, Mr Mayor, the works supervisor will be unable to attend that meeting."

"Why?"

"Because he'll be on holiday, Mr Mayor," replied the Town Clerk. "Marvellous, isn't it?" muttered Tom Gaskell to Jim Sparks, slumped down in the seat beside him. "Benson seems to spend a third of the year sick, a third on holiday and a third drinking tea in Cecil Conway's office. It's a miracle this town doesn't come to a complete halt."

"Well, then, I propose it be put on the agenda of the next full council meeting in a month's time," said the Mayor, impatiently. "All agree?"

A series of grunts and nods affirmed that the council did, indeed, agree. "That appears to be the end of our business, tonight," snapped the Mayor, a glance at his watch showing that the second half of the game was still within his grasp. "Will somebody move the Common Seal?"

"So moved," said Councillor Sparks.

"Thank you," replied the Mayor. "And thank you for your attendance, ladies and gentlemen, I declare the meeting closed at 10.15 pm."

XXXXXXXXXXXX

Frank Jackson called the meeting to order.

"Good evening, Ladies and Gentlemen," he intoned.

"Evening, Mr Mayor," came the mumbling replies.

"We're pleased to welcome the Reverend Gladstone, Vicar of our parish church, to lead us in prayer."

The parson glanced cursorily at the ranks of councillors, and at the half dozen ratepayers - most of them regular attenders - who had come to view and listen to the deliberations of their elected representatives, sadly reflected that the only time he ever saw any of them in church was at funerals, then lowered his head and mouthed his usual call for the Lord to bestow wisdom upon the very mortal members of this council.

The Reverend Gladstone duly said his piece, was thanked by the Mayor, and wasted no time in making good his escape from the chamber. Frank Jackson, meanwhile, was looking at item 2 upon the routinely listed agenda.

"Apologies for absence?"

"I have only one, Mr Mayor," replied Cecil Conway, "from Mrs Gilbert; I'm afraid she's unwell."

"Thank heavens for that," muttered Tom Gaskell to his eternal neighbour, Jim Sparks. "That means there'll be no trees tonight. Be able to get home at a sensible hour."

"She's probably suffering from Dutch Elm disease," whispered Sparks, grinning broadly at his joke.

"Item 3 - Minutes of the meeting of the full council held in this chamber last month. These have been circulated; is it your wish I sign them as a true record?" The Mayor glanced around the chamber, took in the slight movement of hands and a few muttered "ayes," and quickly penned his signature to the bottom of the relevant page, of the large minute ledger.

"Mr Mayor, before you sign the minutes," said Mrs Beckett, getting to her feet, "I would like to question the wording of minute 72."

"You're a bit slow, Mrs Beckett," said the Mayor, sternly. "I've already signed the minutes now as being correct."

"Well, yes, I appreciate that, Mr Mayor, and I'm sorry for not getting up before - my attention was distracted by somebody slamming a door somewhere. It's just that I feel that whilst the minute isn't exactly wrong, its clarity would be greatly improved if in the last line of the minute the word "suggested" was used rather than "proposed"."

"It means the same thing, Mr Mayor," said Tom Gaskell.

"No, it doesn't, Mr Mayor," argued Mrs Beckett, stoically. "There is a subtle difference which I believe would be more in keeping with the subject of this minute. It is, after all, rather sensitive."

"The woman's daft," muttered Jim Sparks. "Imagine wasting the council's time with nonsense like that."

"Imagine reading the minutes," replied Tom Gaskell. "I've been on this council for nearly twenty years and I've never read the minutes yet," he continued, proudly.

"Members agree we change the word as suggested by Mrs

Beckett?" asked the Mayor. He took the grunts to mean that they did agree, and altered the minutes accordingly.

"Item 4 - Matters arising."

"There is none, Mr Mayor," intoned the town clerk.

"Item 5 - verbal report from the Works supervisor concerning the flagpole on top of the town hall tower." The Mayor glanced at the gnarled figure sitting on his left.

"Mr Benson, please."

"Thank you, Mr Mayor," said Billy Benson, his deep, melancholy voice immediately casting its usual pall over the proceedings. A small, rather round-shouldered man in his late fifties, council meetings for him held all the joy of a tooth extraction. His only vision of the future now was to see retirement seductively beckoning him.

"Well, now, about this flagpole. You see........"

"Point of order, Mr Mayor." Councillor Sidney Bartlett, at eighty two, the council's oldest member was on his feet - a rarity in itself.

"Yes, Mr Bartlett?" asked the Mayor, puzzledly.

"It's a very warm night, Mr Mayor. Could we have a couple of windows open please?"

"Yes, of course. Mr Benson before we hear your report, would you open the windows behind you?"

Benson cleared his throat, a little nervously. "Well - er - well I'm afraid I can't open any of the windows, Mr Mayor."

"Why not for heaven's sake?"

"Well, you may remember that back in the Autumn the council decided that the windows should be nailed up to prevent them from being opened because the frames have become rotten. As I recall, Mr Mayor, a small sub-committee was set up to decide future policy as to the windows - whether you wanted double glazing or ordinary windows, UPVC or aluminium frames and so on."

"I don't remember this," rasped the Mayor.

"Mr Benson's quite correct, Mr Mayor," interjected Cecil Conway. "Last October, I think it was, when we decided to set up the sub-committee. I've got it all minuted." He immediately began to toss aside the piles of folders, and sheets of paper, lying mountainously on the desk in front of him. Frank Jackson gazed at him in exasperation - would the day ever dawn when the town clerk found the file he was looking for?

"It doesn't matter about the minutes, Mr Conway - we'll take your word for it," snapped the Mayor, making little effort to disguise the annoyance in his voice.

"I seem to remember something about this, Mr Mayor," said Arthur Phillips. "As I recall, the sub-committee was to meet to decide exactly the kind of windows we wanted for the chamber and then the works supervisor would be able to get estimates of cost. I can't remember who was on the committee though."

"Mayor, Deputy Mayor, Chairman of Properties and Chairman of Finance and General Purpose, Mr Mayor or, at least, that's usual composition of sub-committees," opined Cecil Conway.

"Well, when did this committee meet? I certainly don't remember ever attending or being informed of any of its meetings."

"You would have been informed, Mr Mayor. You would have received an agenda like everybody else," said Conway, urbanely. "Perhaps you overlooked it?"

"It's possible, I suppose," agreed the Mayor. "Anyway, what did the committee decide - and why hasn't it been done?"

"Well, actually, it didn't decide anything Mr Mayor. As I

recall, the first meeting was scheduled for a date in early December but unfortunately it had to be put off because it clashed with the Annual General Meeting of the local Toc H branch."

"What's Toc H got to do with this Council?" asked Arthur Phillips, somewhat bemused.

"Nothing directly, Mr Mayor. It's just that Toc H had booked the council chamber that evening, as I recall, so obviously we couldn't use it for the sub-committee meeting. However, we did put forward an new date for mid-January, but as members will recall, the very cold weather caused the central heating system in this building to freeze so we had to postpone that meeting as well. For some reason, the setting of a further date for a meeting of the committee has been overlooked, Mr Mayor."

"Meaning that the town clerk overlooked it, Mr Mayor," snapped Arthur Phillips, who always got belligerent in the hot weather.

"I must protest at that, Mr Mayor. I merely obey instructions from the council. I received no further instructions as to when members wished the meeting to take place. However, I did foresee some major work being done on the windows of this chamber, so ensured that a sum of money was put by in the estimates to cover it."

"How much?" asked Jim Sparks.

"A thousand pounds," replied Conway.

"A thousand pounds," roared Sparks, "Mr Mayor, that wouldn't cover the cost of the sills in windows of this size. We'll be lucky if we get this job done for less than £15,000."

"Then there's no chance of doing it, Mr Mayor," retorted Conway, tartly. "This authority doesn't have that sort of money to spend."

"It seems to me that we're getting nowhere fast on this issue," said Frank Jackson "The fact is that we're facing the Summer without being able to open the windows. I don't know who's directly to blame for this, and I don't really care. All I know is, something has to be done - and done quickly."

"That's all very well, Mr Mayor, but we're obviously talking about a lot of money being spent on these windows," said Tom Gaskell. "I feel we've a duty to the chargepayers not to rush into anything, but to ensure that at the end of the day we get value for money."

"I agree with Councillor Gaskell, Mr Mayor," said Jim Sparks, authoritively, "and with that in mind, I propose that this entire matter be referred to the next meeting of the Properties Committee for further discussion."

"I second that," said Gaskell.

"Very well," said the Mayor, with a sigh - too hot in his rather heavy suit to contemplate having an argument. "All those in favour." The motion was carried.

"Now perhaps we can let Mr Benson get on with telling us about the problems he's got with the flagpole."

"Thank you, Mr Mayor," said Benson mournfully. "You see, the trouble with the flagpole is that it's rotten, especially the top half. That's the trouble with wood, of course - rot. Most flagpoles these days are made of metal. That's what I would recommend the council goes for next time when the pole is replaced. And it'll have to be replaced obviously; it's beyond repair."

"That's all very well, Mr Mayor," interjected Nigel Hollins, "but the works supervisor's still not told us how the two flags in question came to be flying at half mast."

"Well, that's simple enough, Mr Mayor," replied the phlegmatic official. "You see, the wood at the top is so rotten it won't hold the nails, which hold the pulley wheel in place, any longer. When we came to pull the French flag up on the morning of the day Mr Hollins is complaining about, the nails just came away and the pulley fell off. We tried to nail it back in place, but we were halfway down the pole before we found wood sound enough to take the nails. So that's why the flag looked to be at half mast."

"It didn't look to be, Mr Mayor," retorted Hollins, "It was."

"Well, yes, I suppose it was, Mr Mayor," agreed Benson. "And the same thing happened with the Queen's Birthday, of course."

"So what are we going to do about it?" asked Arthur Phillips.

"Well, of course, we'll have to have a new flagpole - as I said just now," replied Benson.

"Obviously so," said the Mayor. "And I reckon we want one as soon as possible. I feel, Councillors, that we should instruct the Works Supervisor to get a new one as soon as possible."

"How much will it cost, Mr Mayor?" asked Jim Sparks.

The Mayor glanced questioningly at Billy Benson.

"Well, Mr Mayor, I've not had a firm estimate, but I have had a word with a couple of builders in the town and they tell me it'll cost between...." he coughed nervously, and looked down at the desk in front of him; "between twelve hundred and fifteen hundred pounds."

"What? Did - did the works supervisor say twelve to fifteen hundred pounds, Mr Mayor?"

"That's what it sounded like to me, Mr Sparks."

"But that's ridiculous. How can it cost money like that? After all, it's only a piece of metal about fifteen feet long," rasped Sparks.

"It's not the cost of the actual flagpole, Mr Mayor," replied Benson. "That wouldn't be any great price at all. It's the erection of it which causes the problems - and eats up the money. You see, although we can maintain the pole from the top of the tower, and put the flags on, of course, when it comes to replacing the pole, it necessitates scaffolding - and that costs a fortune."

"But why, Mr Mayor?" asked Arthur Phillips.

Billy Benson looked at the councillor in his rather squint-eyed way. "It just does, Mr Mayor. These scaffolding firms charge a great deal to erect it all, and then charge it out at a fair old fee for each day."

"I wasn't referring to the scaffolding," snorted Phillips testily. "I know that costs a fortune. What I want to know is why we need scaffolding to start with - why the job can't be done from the top of the tower?"

"It's all to do with the siting of the pole, Mr Mayor. Because of the construction of the top of the tower, the flagpole cannot be erected on the actual roof. Instead, it's cemented down against the side of the tower - as many councillors no doubt realize - which means we have to have scaffolding, I'm afraid."

Councillor Jack Dawson pulled himself slowly to his feet and gazed vaguely in the direction of the "chair", through his pebble glasses, "Mr Mayor, instead of talking about spending a small fortune on a new flagpole, why don't we continue to use the one we've got?"

"Because it's rotten for heaven's sake," retorted Nigel Hollins. "What do you think we've been talking about for the past ten minutes?"

"Only the top half's rotten - the rest isn't," continued Dawson, doggedly. "If the top half was cut off, then we could use the lower half as a flagpole, Mr Mayor. It would probably last for another ten years like that."

"Mr Mayor, we can't have flags flying from half a flagpole. Why it would be - well, demeaning for the town. And an insult to those we were supposed to be honouring by flying their flag," insisted Hollins.

"I must agree with you there, Mr Hollins," said the Mayor.

"I agree it would look daft flying flags from half a flagpole, Mr Mayor, but surely the easiest solution is to do away with a flagpole altogether," said Tom Gaskell.

"We must have a flagpole, Mr Mayor," said Mrs Beckett.

"Why?" asked Gaskell.

"Because we must. Every town has an official flagpole - some more than one. In fact every village, and probably even some hamlets, have official flagpoles. There are many important occasions which need to be marked by the flying of flags. To say, Mr Mayor, that we should do away with the flagpole altogether is absurd."

"Not so, Mr Mayor," insisted the tenacious Tom Gaskell. "That flagpole is the most underused piece of council property in this town. We fly the French flag when the Frogs are over here on their annual twinning booze up, the Stars and Stripes on Independence Day - though why, is beyond me - and the Union Jack on the Queen's Birthday and a couple of other occasions. An expenditure of fifteen hundred pence would be too great for that amount of use, let alone fifteen hundred pounds."

"Mr Gaskell is being parochial and, with respect, somewhat petty minded about this, Mr Mayor," opined Nigel Hollins. "The flying of flags of various nations over the town hall of this town is a very important aspect of the vital work of cementing relationships between ourselves and countries throughout Europe - the world in fact. And there have been many more national flags than those which Mr Gaskell has named flown from that flagpole during recent years."

"Like the time we flew the East German flag to welcome the West German delegation who came to discuss a possible twinning link a few years back," snorted Jim Sparks. "No wonder we've never heard a word from them since."

"That was a most unfortunate error, Mr Mayor," said Hollins, quickly, "due to the fact that our letter requesting a flag was sent to the wrong embassy in London." He fixed the town clerk with a somewhat malevolent glare, before returning his gaze to the "chair."

"May I ask the works supervisor, through you, Mr Mayor, if our own council staff could be used to replace the flagpole. That would save some money, surely."

"No chance, Mr Mayor, I'm afraid," said Benson, shaking his head solemnly. "This is obviously a tradesman's job, and we've only got two tradesmen, Gordon Lashman and Henry Collins. Unfortunately, Mr Lashman, who's not far off retirement as councillors will probably be aware, suffers rather badly from asthma and would find it impossible to climb all those internal steps leading to the roof of the tower, whilst Mr Collins can't stand heights. No, there's no way we can use our own labour."

"Then is there no possible way, Mr Mayor?" asked Mrs Beckett, "that the flagpole can be replaced without the use of scaffolding; or, at least, extensive scaffolding. That obviously is where the expense lies."

Billy Benson looked somewhat dubious, then shrugged his shoulders. "I'm doubtful, Mr Mayor," he said, "but there is a remote possibility that it could be done in a different way -

which would save us a lot of money."

"That being?"

"Well, there's a builder in the town - I hadn't better mention his name because I haven't been able to get hold of him, as he's on holiday in Canada - who's also a trained steeplejack. Now on a couple of occasions I've known him avoid the use of scaffolding by donning a kind of safety harness and hanging over the side of one or two buildings in the town. I know that he replaced some missing slates on a high part of the church roof using this method. He's never done any work for the council, but then we've never needed this kind of specialist work done before. Whether he could use this harness method to replace the flagpole I obviously don't know, but I will certainly ask him when he returns from holiday."

"When will that be?" asked the Mayor.

"He's away for over two months, Mr Mayor. Not due back until the end of June, so his sister told me when I was talking to her a few days ago. Still, I can certainly have a word with him as soon as he returns and then report to the July meeting of the full council."

"That sounds fair enough, Mr Benson," agreed the Mayor. "There's no great panic about this job, although the sooner it's done the better of course. But if hanging on a couple of months is going to save us a sizeable amount of money, then it will be well worth while. Members agree that we await a report along these lines at the July meeting?" Mumbled "ayes" and grunts of assent ruled the day.

XXXXXXXXXXXX

The July meeting agreed to the planting, suggested by Mrs

Gilbert, of a further fifty trees, decided to write a letter of protest to the county council - and the local MP - at their decision to sell off half the playing fields of the local comprehensive school for building, and donated fifty pounds towards a new roof for the town's citizens advice bureau. As to the flagpole, nothing was done because Billy Benson's mysterious steeplejack was so enjoying himself in Canada that he decided to stay for a further month, thus returning at the end of July. As the council stood in recess throughout August, it was agreed that Benson should report to the September meeting of the council.

XXXXXXXXXXXX

The September meeting was held on a very cool evening, much to the relief of both Cecil Conway and Billy Benson, neither of whom had made any real progress towards bringing windows to the chamber which would open. The holiday break seemed to have done everybody a power of good, for the meeting moved along at a brisk pace, the members exuding an air of efficiency. It was agreed that a further part-time worker be appointed to help keep the cemetery tidy, and the grass mowed - Mrs Crosby's objection that it was a silly time to appoint anybody extra to the outdoor staff as there would soon be no grass to mow thanks to winter frosts, being over-ruled.

"We do need time to train a man to handle the mowers and such like, Mr Mayor," pointed out Cecil Conway, "so if he is appointed now, then come next Spring, he'll be most proficient in all his duties."

This argument didn't convince anybody, but it was generally thought an extra pair of hands - albeit part-time - throughout the Winter would be useful in order to improve the general standard of the cemetery.

The meeting voted to write to the county council, with a copy to the local MP, complaining about the state of the main street of the town - "there're pot holes there so big they've got their own wildlife," as Jim Sparks put it - and a letter was also to be sent to the district council complaining about the deplorable state of the public conveniences. "I suspect that the public lavatories in the slums of Calcutta are kept better than ours, Mr Mayor," as Mrs Beckett put it, rather dramatically.

Tom Gaskell, who'd travelled large portions of the world during his ten years as a merchant sailor, informed the council in general, and Mrs Beckett in particular, that having once visited Calcutta, he could categorically state that whilst there was considerable room for improvement in the general upkeep of the town lavatories, they were still somewhat better than those found in the sprawling Indian port. Mrs Beckett, at her formidable best, took issue with Gaskell upon the subject, but was eventually silenced when the Mayor demanded it by slamming down his gavel.

The last item on the agenda, before "any other business", was entered: "Town Hall flagpole. To determine a course of action."

The Mayor glanced at Billy Benson. "As I recall, Mr Benson, you were going to have a word with this builder, steeplejack fellow you know when he returned from Canada, and see if he could tackle the renewal of the flagpole without scaffolding."

"Yes, that's right, Mr Mayor" replied the works supervisor, getting stiffly to his feet. "Well, this chap came home at the beginning of last month, so I've been able to discuss the matter with him. And I'm glad to say the news is good - he can renew the flagpole using a safety harness which suspends him from the top of the tower. This means, of course, he'll not need any scaffolding, so the price will be radically less than the twelve to fifteen hundred pounds mentioned recently."

"How much less?" asked Arthur Phillips.

"This chap reckons it'll cost about four hundred pounds, including the price of the flagpole."

"Mr Mayor," interjected Jim Sparks, "we're treating this steeplejack as if his name's secret. Is there any reason why we cannot know exactly who we're talking about?"

The Mayor shook his head. "None as far as I'm aware, Mr Sparks. This fellow wouldn't mind having his name made public I assume, Mr Benson?"

"No - no, I shouldn't think so, Mr Mayor. Obviously there's no secret involved in all this. For members information, the chap I'm thinking of is Colin Matthews who lives in Holly Close. He's a good tradesman from what I've heard, and I'm sure will be just the fellow we need to sort out this flagpole business."

"If we give the go ahead, how soon can he begin the job?" asked Nigel Hollins.

"Almost immediately," replied Benson. "He's just got a small job to finish, which'll not take him more than a couple of days apparently, then he's got a few days spare before he starts some biggish job somewhere in the town. He reckons our job'll not take more than a couple of days at the outside."

"That sounds excellent, Mr Mayor," said Hollins. "It would mean that we'd have a new flagpole in place long before the end of the month - when we're expecting a visit from the folk dance group of Pontville sur la Mer. We'd be able to fly the tricolour in a proper fashion this time."

"Not another blasted twinning effort," muttered Tom Gaskell. "If the chargepayers knew how much money was wasted on all this nonsense, they'd sack the lot of us."

"No they wouldn't," whispered Jim Sparks in reply. "I'd soon see to it that everybody knew it was Hollins' folly not ours."

"So it's members wishes that we instruct the works supervisor to ask Mr Matthews to replace the flagpole as soon as possible?"

"With a metal one, of course, Mr Mayor," interjected Mrs Crosby.

"Naturally," replied Frank Jackson. "All those in favour, please show."

"Just a minute, Mr Mayor," wheezed Sidney Bartlett, pulling himself to his feet. "I fancy we're out of order on this one, you know."

"In what way, Mr Bartlett?"

"Well it says in standing orders that if any building or maintenance work is going to cost more than fifty pounds, then we have to go out to tender. We're talking here of four hundred pounds - and it could be more; after all, we've not had a proper estimate from this fellow."

Frank Jackson nodded, "That's a very fair point, Mr Bartlett - and one which I'd not considered, I must confess."

Cecil Conway sprang to his feet. "I'm afraid Mr Bartlett is somewhat out of date, Mr Mayor. There probably was a fifty pound limit some years ago - though I must say it was before my time - but the limit now is two hundred and fifty pounds."

"Which still means we've got to put it out to tender, Mr Mayor," rasped Tom Gaskell.

"Mr Bartlett's quite right. I don't know how the town clerk failed to advise us of this in the first place. If we go ahead with this at present, without others being given the chance to tender, then the district auditor will be down on us like a ton of bricks. In fact, we could end up in jail."

"All, that is, except the town clerk," muttered Jim Sparks.

"With respect, Mr Mayor," replied Cecil Conway, "I do think Mr Gaskell is exaggerating somewhat. Certainly the district auditor would ask questions if we contemplated spending into four figures without going to tender, but I hardly think he'll call the fraud squad in for a mere one hundred and fifty pounds over our official limit." He smiled his patient smile at the council and resumed his seat.

"That's all very well, Mr Mayor," retorted Bartlett, doggedly, "but standing orders are the rules by which this council operates, and those rules should be obeyed - to the letter. If we start ignoring them here, and bending them there, where'll we all end up?"

"I agree with Councillor Bartlett, Mr Mayor," said Tom Gaskell. "These things have got to be done properly."

"But if we go through all the palaver of putting it out to tender, it'll put the replacement of the flagpole back weeks - in fact, months probably, Mr Mayor," whined Nigel Hollins.

"He's worried that he won't be able to raise the Tricolour when the Frogs come over at the end of the month," muttered Jim Sparks to Gaskell.

"That's just too bad, Mr Mayor," retorted Tom Gaskell, springing to his feet once again. "As I said just now, these things have got to be done properly. And it's not as if there's any real urgency to the matter. I'm sure we can carry on as we are for the time being."

"Mr Mayor, we cannot continue to fly flags at half mast," observed Douglas Denny.

"Quite right, Mr Mayor," said Jack Dawson. "But if the council adopted the idea that I put forward in a previous meeting, we could use the existing flagpole until another is erected, and the flags would not be at half mast."

"What idea was that, Mr Dawson?"

"To cut the top half off the pole and just use the bottom, Mr Mayor," retorted Dawson sharply, a touch of hurt in his voice, motivated by the fact that Frank Jackson had forgotten his wise remarks of a couple of months earlier.

"Well, yes, that would appear to be a reasonable plan - in the short term," agreed the Mayor.

"Yes, quite so, Mr Mayor," agreed Arthur Phillips. "If Councillor Dawson is making it a proposition that we cut the top off the pole and use the bottom half until we put up a new one, then I second it."

"Do you propose that, Mr Dawson?"

"Yes, I suppose I do, Mr Mayor. I fancy it's a good short term solution. In the meantime tenders can be invited for the erection of the new flagpole - including one from Mr Matthews. I know he said about four hundred pounds, but I really do think it needs to be put down on paper - from everybody's point of view."

"I agree, Mr Dawson. You've heard the proposal, councillors; I believe you're going to second it, Mr Phillips?"

"Yes - I second the proposal, Mr Mayor," agreed Phillips.

"All in favour, please show - carried," droned the Mayor, not taking a lot of notice as to who was, or wasn't, voting in favour of the motion. He turned to the town clerk.

"Will you be able to get tenders in sufficiently quickly to be able to bring them to the next meeting, Mr Conway?"

"What, you mean the next meeting of the council, Mr Mayor?"

"He gets dafter by the minute - what does he think we mean, the next meeting of the Fatstock Show Committee?" muttered Jim Sparks.

"Of course," retorted the Mayor, "what other organisation are you in the habit of reporting to?"

"Well - quite, Mr Mayor. But what I was meaning was whether you wished me to report to the full council or the Properties Committee. It would, of course, be correct procedure to report to the Properties Committee."

"Quite so. In that case, bring the tenders to them. I'm sure that would be in order, Mrs Crosby - wouldn't it?"

The Chairman of the Properties Committee nodded. "Yes, Mr Mayor," she agreed. "and perhaps we could be given delegated powers to accept the lowest tender and put the work in hand. After all, if we have to wait for the full council to meet, then we'll waste another week."

"That makes sense," agreed Frank Jackson. "Are members in agreement to delegate powers to the Properties Committee to take this action?"

"Just a moment, Mr Mayor, please," interjected Cecil Conway. "I've just been thinking that whilst everything proposed certainly makes sense, there is the possibility that all the tenders might not be in by the time of the Properties Committee meeting."

"They will if you make the deadline a few days before the Committee is due to meet," pointed out Mrs Crosby.

"Well - yes, true. But that doesn't really give those tendering much time to work out their estimates, does it? I feel it's just a little unfair on them. With that in mind, perhaps it would be better if I bring the tenders to the meeting of the full council, the week afterwards, Mr Mayor."

"We're going round in circles as usual," muttered Jim Sparks.

"Yes, all right - the full council," rapped the Mayor testily, rapidly becoming fed-up with the entire business. "Members agree that the tenders be brought to the next meeting of this council?"

Members did, indeed, agree.

XXXXXXXXXXXX

Amongst other matters, it was agreed at the October meeting of the Council that Colin Matthews' tender of £425 for the providing and erecting of a flagpole on top of the town hall tower be accepted, the work to be put in hand immediately. His wasn't the lowest tender - it was the only tender.

XXXXXXXXXXXX

At the November meeting, Billy Benson revealed in his customary monthly report on the general maintenance work being carried out on council property, that Mr Matthews had, as yet, been unable to make a start on the erection of the new flagpole owing to the fact that he'd had a small accident.

"Does this fellow ever do any work?" asked Tom Gaskell. "It seems to me he's either abroad on holiday or sick."

The Mayor admonished him for the remarks. "Mr Gaskell, these are rather personal comments and whilst I appreciate you're saying them - well, perhaps 'tongue in cheek' would be the best way to describe it - they're still remarks which could be misconstrued, and should be kept out of open council."

"Who said I made them 'tongue in cheek'" muttered the unrepentant Gaskell to Jim Sparks.

"Apparently, Mr Mayor, Mr Matthews was just a bit unlucky," explained the works supervisor. "He told me that he descended a ladder from which he was working in Fore Street the very day before he was due to make a start on the flagpole, and as his right foot hit the pavement at the bottom of the ladder, he stumbled rather badly, and fell off the edge of the pavement breaking a small bone in his foot in the process."

"He sounds like a right star," muttered Gaskell once again. "After all, how do you fall off a ladder when you're on the bottom rung?"

"How long will he be off work, Mr Benson?" asked the Mayor.

"Until about Christmas, Mr Mayor. He told me on the phone this morning, when I enquired as to his progress, that he'll definitely be starting work again in the New Year."

"That's quite sometime, Mr Mayor," said Nigel Hollins, "perhaps we should consider getting somebody else to do the job."

Arthur Phillips jumped to his feet. "That's ridiculous, Mr Mayor!" he cried. "By the time we go through all the business of going out to tender, and so on, and getting replies in, Matthews will have had enough time to get over a heart transplant, let alone a cracked bone in the foot. Anyway, nobody'll tender for the job, will they? - except to do it the expensive way using scaffolding. No, it'll be a lot quicker to wait for this fellow to recover."

Frank Jackson nodded his agreement. "I fancy you're right, Mr Phillips, and I'm sure most members will agree."

Most members did, indeed, agree.

XXXXXXXXXXXX

The subject of the flagpole was not a particularly burning issue at the January meeting of the council, several other problems having supplanted it in the consciousness of councillors. Principal amongst these was the vandalising of the town hall ladies' cloakroom over the Christmas period, the discovery of dry rot in the Mayor's parlour, situated at the back of the council chamber and the threat by the amateur operatic society to sue the council over the partial collapse of the town hall stage, with them stood on it, during their annual Christmas carol concert. However, at the end of a long verbal report, the works supervisor did state that, unfortunately, owing to the bad weather, work had not yet started on erecting the new flagpole.

"What bad weather, Mr Mayor?" asked Nigel Hollins, genuine puzzlement upon his face. "My wife only remarked to me this morning how mild the weather is for the time of year."

"Well - yes, that's true to a degree, Mr Mayor," agreed Benson solemnly. "But it's still been rather wet and cold - not very nice weather to be working at the top of that tower."

"Of course it's been wet and cold, Mr Mayor," rasped Jim Sparks. "It's always like that in January. Come to that, it's usually like that in June around here. If this fellow Matthews isn't going aloft to do this job until the weather's perfect then I reckon Mr Gaskell here will have his way after all - the flagpole will never be replaced."

"It's not quite like that, Mr Mayor," replied Benson, stoically. "All Mr Matthews is waiting for are a couple of reasonably dry, frost-free days. There's cement involved in this job, you know. It's impossible to cement around the base of the pole, down the side of the tower, unless the weather is reasonable."

"Yes, fair point, Mr Benson," interjected Frank Jackson quickly. The meeting had already dragged on quite long enough

- and there were highlights of the FA Cup replays on the box in less than half an hour. "Let's hope the weather improves sufficiently for the job to be done before our next meeting."

Billy Benson most earnestly shared the Mayor's hope.

Late January and the early part of February brought some unseasonably sunny weather - but little joy for Benson. Indeed, the February meeting of the council saw the hapless works supervisor face a torrid time. Escalating dry rot, and costs to match; the vandalising of the town hall ladies' cloakroom being followed by like treatment of the gents; the operatic society threatening to sue him personally as well as the council - were just some of the problems which were making his life a misery. And Arthur Phillips didn't help matters, for at his insistence a date had been fixed for a meeting of the sub committee which was to consider the state, and replacement, of the chamber windows - despite a masterly attempt at prevarication by Cecil Conway. Still, he was winning. He only had one final item on his list of work done - or about to be done, sometime - and the meeting would be virtually over.

"Concerning the flagpole, Mr Mayor," he said, gazing steadfastly down at the top of his desk, "I'm afraid we've run into a bit of a snag."

"Not another one, Mr Mayor?" roared an angry Nigel Hollins, jumping to his feet. "Damn it all, the Egyptians built pyramids quicker than it's taking us to replace that infernal flagpole. I thought this builder was supposed to be a steeplejack - and used to doing work like this?"

"Well, it's not really his fault, Mr Mayor," replied Benson. "The problem lies with the flagpole itself. Mr Matthews put the work in hand a couple of weeks back when the drier weather came, as he said he would. It only took him a day to take down the remaining part of the old flagpole and prepare for the new one, and at the end of the afternoon he told me that he would erect the new one the following day. The next morning, though, when he inspected the new pole before hoisting it aloft, he noticed a very slight crack in the alloy - and decided it wouldn't be safe to erect it. He said that if it was put up in that condition there would always be a chance that it would snap in a gale, and, of course, come hurtling down into the street. Obviously the council can't take that sort of risk, so the flagpole has been sent back to the suppliers and we're awaiting a new one."

"And how long will that take?" demanded the irate Hollins.

"Well, unfortunately the suppliers had no further flagpoles in stock," replied the works supervisor, "so they've had to send to the factory for another one. They reckoned at the time that delivery would be about a month or so. This was about a fortnight ago, so it should be here in roughly another fortnight."

"A month, Mr Mayor, just to get another flagpole. What are they using to transport this piece of metal - a mule?" Nigel Hollins was in a mood to draw blood.

"No - a ship, Mr Mayor."

"Why a ship?" asked Hollins.

"Because it has to come from South Korea," replied Benson, totally without emotion.

"You have to be joking," roared Hollins, rolling his eyes towards the ceiling. "Surely they can get a simple alloy flagpole a little closer than South Korea, Mr Mayor?"

"Apparently not, Mr Mayor, it seems that this kind of pole - which, incidentally, should last a good twenty-five years - isn't made in this country at all," replied Benson.

"Twenty-five years?" rasped Tom Gaskell. "It'll take that long to have the blasted thing erected as far as I can see, Mr

Mayor."

"I do sympathise with what you say, Mr Gaskell," replied the Mayor, "but sadly these things do happen - as they say. Hopefully, we'll soon take delivery of a new pole and it will be up there on top of the tower by the time we next meet."

"I wouldn't back that with a lot of money," muttered Jim Sparks.

"What I want to know, Mr Mayor, is why the defect in this flagpole wasn't discovered far earlier?" said Mrs Beckett. "After all, I would imagine, seeing as this job was supposed to be done months ago, that it's been in our possession for some considerable time."

"Not in our possession, Mr Mayor," interjected the works supervisor, rare urgency in his voice. "No, it's never been in our possession. As the contractor, the obtaining of the flagpole - like all the other materials - is the responsibility of Mr Matthews."

"Well, how long has it been in his possession, then?" persisted Mrs Beckett.

"I don't really know," replied Benson, "but I think he's had it several months."

"Then why didn't he discover this defect before?" Alison Beckett was not a woman to shirk her duty of ascertaining the truth when she suspected incompetence.

"I obviously can't say, Mr Mayor," said Billy Benson, a little wearily. "Perhaps it's only just developed this fault," he added lamely.

"I can't accept that, Mr Mayor," said the good lady. "I'm no expert on metals, but I find it hard to believe that defects can suddenly appear in an unused alloy flagpole - just like that. It seems to me that this flagpole was delivered to Mr Matthews in a defective condition, and this fault was only discovered months later. Incompetence, Mr Mayor - that's what this is. I'm not at all sure that this contractor is the right one to be entrusted with the erection of a new flagpole on the town hall tower."

"Mr Mayor, don't let us go over this ground again!" cried Jim Sparks. "This entire business seems to be taking an eternity as it is, so for heaven's sake don't let us do anything which is going to drag it out even longer. I agree that this flagpole should have been checked months ago, but the fact is, it hasn't, so there's nothing we can do about that. The important thing now, though, Mr Mayor, is that a new one's on order and should be delivered in a fortnight. Then, with just a little bit of luck, the blasted thing will be erected on top of the tower and we can start flying flags again in a way which won't upset half the ratepayers of this town - and most of the visitors. So no more talk of getting a new contractor or anything like that; if we go along that road we'll all be in our dotage before the job's done."

"Yes, I must agree with you, Mr Sparks," said the Mayor, nodding sagely. "I think we must stick with Mr Matthews and hope that this new flagpole is soon delivered - and erected. Members agree?"

Members - or most of them - did, indeed, agree.

XXXXXXXXXXXX

Frank Jackson looked at his watch; it was dragging on once again. He couldn't remember the last time he'd attended a brief council meeting. Here it was, nearly ten o'clock and there was still a good half hour left in it yet. It was Jack Dawson's fault this time - as it always was at the March meeting. Not habitually a man to myther on unless he really had something to say, Jack, nonetheless, always went to town about any expenditure on the bowling green; and March was when Cecil Conway always itemised the things which needed to be done to bring the green up to its traditionally excellent standard - and their cost.

Nobody knew why Dawson so resented any expenditure on the green - and consequent help to the bowling club - but throughout the fifteen years he'd been on the council, he'd stood up at every March meeting and made a verbose, almost passionate, appeal to his fellow councillors to cut back radically on the spending of ratepayers money on the green, and bowling club. This appeal usually led to a protracted debate, the statement from Sidney Bartlett that the bowling green was "the jewel in the town's crown", and invariably, an overwhelming vote in favour of maintaining the green to the usual standard. And Jack Dawson would always demand of the town clerk that his name be recorded in the minutes as voting against it.

This night was no exception, although the debate went on even longer than usual. Perhaps "debate" would be a rather inaccurate word to use, as it gives the impression of a number of people each contributing something different in the way of ideas and opinions to the discussion. Regarding the bowling green, however, it was a case of Jack Dawson on one side and the rest of the council on the other, with most members virtually repeating what had already been said. Still, Frank Jackson - probably the most patient Mayor the town had had in years - rationalised it in his mind, as he sat in his imposing-looking chair gazing down at his verbally marauding fellow councillors, as being "democracy at work."

Jack Dawson's March madness was bad enough, but Mrs Gilbert had chosen this meeting as well to talk about trees - as she did at great length about four times a year. This time she suggested that an arboretum be created in a corner of the park, and painstakingly listed the twenty-five different species of tree which she felt should be bought by the Council to fill it. And once again, she insisted on using the Latin names. Her monologue would have gone on even longer than it did, but Jim Sparks saved the day by interrupting her as she was about to list a dozen or so different varieties of shrub which she felt would look nice planted close to the arboretum.

"I'm sure there is much merit in Mrs Gilbert's ideas and suggestions, Mr Mayor," said Sparks, "but I feel that such matters should be looked at more closely and, perhaps, our entire policy towards tree planting brought up to date. With that in mind, I propose this matter be referred to the next meeting of the Properties Committee." This wasn't the first time Jim Sparks had used such a ploy to stop Mrs Gilbert in full flood, nor was it the first time it had succeeded. Councillors wished to get home tonight.

"I second Mr Spark's proposal, Mr Mayor," interjected Tom Gaskell quickly.

"All those in favour, please show," said the Mayor, entering into the spirit of haste. "Carried - the question of tree planting for this year, and future years, will be put on the agenda of the next Properties Committee."

"Must make a point of missing that one," muttered Jim Sparks to Tom Gaskell.

"Me as well," agreed Gaskell.

For Billy Benson, it was the easiest meeting he'd known in a long time - largely because his report was almost positive. The town hall dry rot had largely been sorted out but there had been vandalism to the children's slide in the park. However, the youth who did it had fallen off the slide whilst trying to rip up the boards of the platform at the top, and broken a leg. He had been charged with criminal damage by the police, Benson reported with satisfaction to an attentive council.

"Birch the bugger," rasped Arthur Phillips, "that's what they should do."

"I beg your pardon, Mr Phillips?" inquired the Mayor.

"Corporal punishment, Mr Mayor, that's the answer," was Phillips modified comment.

The Mayor had been that way before when the seemingly eternal problem of vandalism was discussed - seemingly eternally. "We shall just have to let the law take its course, Mr Phillips," he said urbanely, and totally inadequately, something he was as aware of as the rest of the council.

Billy Benson further informed the council that although the town swimming pool contained a leak - as it had for the past ten years - thanks to the remedial work carried out during the Autumn and Winter, it was certainly leaking less than in previous years.

"I'm sure councillors will be pleased to hear this, Mr Mayor," he said, almost with enthusiasm.

Members were, indeed, pleased to hear this. Any news, even minimally good, concerning the swimming pool was greeted with delight, it having a great rarity value. Members, though, didn't pursue any discussion on the continuing leaks - after all, the less said about the swimming pool, the better for all of them.

The works supervisor moved on to the last item on his list, and came close to smiling when he mentioned it - a rare thing indeed.

"The new flagpole has been erected, Mr Mayor, and is all ready to - to - well, to receive flags."

"That is good news, Mr Benson," said the Mayor, stealing a

further glance at his watch, and wincing as he saw the hands pointing to 10.35 pm. "I'm sure members will be very pleased to hear this."

Members were, indeed, very pleased to hear such news.

### XXXXXXXXXXXX

Billy Benson gazed morosely out across the serried ranks of motleyed councillors from his seat to the left of the Mayor. To think he had another three years of all this before he could retire on full pension. There might be a way, though, that he could go out through ill health. Scores seemed to do it and get away with it. And he'd felt a little 'peeky' lately. He had not the slightest doubt, though, that he'd feel more than 'peeky' before this evening was out.

As if he didn't have enough problems, for yet more dry rot had been discovered in the town hall - in the kitchens this time and the swimming pool was leaking like a colander again, with the water heating system on the blink, for good measure; and somebody, somehow, had written graffiti on the walls of the Mayor's parlour - how that had happened, when only official guests were ever admitted to the place, he really did not know. Still, at the end of the day, he'd be able to talk his way out of it all - it wasn't, after all, directly his fault that these problems had arisen. It was the other thing which would really make him look an idiot; in fact, he could see some of the more vindictive members of the council - those who had little faith in him as works supervisor - really going to town on it. And he'd have to mention it in his report - that's if it wasn't mentioned by somebody before. After all, someone would have noticed, or been told about it, for sure. There'd certainly been enough phone calls to

Cecil Conway about it.

Benson was right about his ability to fend off, like a veteran opening batsman, the fast bowls directed at him regarding town hall, swimming pool and Mayor's parlour, all these issues being raised as Mrs Crosby, the chairman, read out the minutes of the Properties Committee. He was, though, taken by surprise by the 'bouncer' bowled by Douglas Denny. He knew such a ball had to come sometime during the course of the meeting, but was hoping that he'd be able to fend it off by being able to bring the subject up initially, whilst delivering his monthly report later in the meeting. Denny, though, who considered the works supervisor to be an overpaid incompetent, bowled for the head - and drew blood. As Mrs Crosby presented a minute concerning repair to the door at the foot of the town hall tower, Councillor Denny rose to his feet.

"Concerning the town hall tower, Mr Mayor," he said evenly. "If I might hang a hat, as the saying goes. It was pointed out to me this morning, by an irate ratepayer, that a couple of days ago - the Queen's birthday - no flag was flying from our new flagpole. I did intend to take this up with the town clerk or the works supervisor before this meeting, but unfortunately business delayed me out of town until late afternoon, so I've only been able to get here just in time for the meeting. Mr Mayor, after much blood, sweat and tears we finally got a new flagpole erected on top of the tower because the previous one was rotten. We spent over four hundred pounds and a lot of council hours on the damned thing and what happens on one of the major - possibly, *the* major - flag raising days of the year? why, simply, no sign of the Union Jack. This council, and the ratepayers of this town, demand an explanation, Mr Mayor."

Cecil Conway slid down into his chair, glanced at the Mayor, then at the works supervisor. Frank Jackson looked to his left - at Billy Benson.

"After all the problems we've had obtaining a new flagpole, then getting it erected, Mr Benson, the council does require some good explanation as to why the Union Jack was not raised on the Queen's Birthday," said the Mayor, rare authority in his voice. Billy Benson got to his feet and gazed blearily over the top of the council members at the back wall of the chamber. "Well, Mr Mayor, a - well, a slight - well, problem, has arisen," he stuttered.

"You're not saying," snapped Tom Gaskell, jumping to his feet, "that the flagpole's defective already."

"Well - no, Mr Mayor," replied the hapless works supervisor, "the flagpole's all right."

"What's the problem, then, for heaven's sake," rasped the impatient Jim Sparks.

"The problem, Mr Mayor" replied Benson slowly, still gazing fixedly at the far wall, "is quite simple really - though rather annoying....." He cleared his throat noisily. "The problem is that somebody has stolen our Union Jack."

-------------------

# THE CHAPEL OF REST

Alan Burton dropped his pen onto his notebook, sighed audibly, and leant back in his rather uncomfortable chair. A fine waste of time this was proving to be. It was somewhat unusual though, he had to admit that. Martin Mullins, editor of the 'Bowminster Clarion', had suggested to his deputy editor - and only full-time reporter - that he take in the monthly meeting of the Brendon Coombe Parish Council.

"It's worth a go, Alan," he'd said that afternoon. "There's usually something going on out at Brendon Coombe. In fact, the council out there has rescued more 'news drought' weeks than any other organisation I know. To be honest, I've usually had better and meatier stories from there than I've ever had from Bowminster Town Council meetings. Last night I didn't get a single real story from them - as you know. So we're desperate for something this week. If you can't get anything from Brendon Coombe tonight, then we'll have to lead with the story of the vicar breaking his leg when he fell off a ladder cleaning his windows, and fill up with pictures of Langham village carnival."

"That'll take a bit of doing," retorted Burton, with a laugh. "They only had three floats and one of them couldn't parade through the village because it had a puncture right at the start."

"True - but we can put in a picture of the carnival queen."

"What - the one that's boss-eyed?"

"The very same. Well, she can't help that, can she? And somebody loves her, for sure. But then we won't have to fill very much at all if you can bring in a good story or two from the meeting tonight. Always been a good place for a bit of scandal and jiggery pokery, has Brendon Coombe."

Alan Burton looked blankly at the far wall of the ante-room of Brendon Coombe Parish Hall. Martin Mullins was usually right about things, but tonight was an exception. There appeared to be no sign of the slightest scandal or minutest dire deed at this meeting. In fact, he couldn't recall a more boring council meeting. It took a very protracted discussion - lasting over half an hour - during which all eleven members of the council spoke, for them to decide, on the casting vote of the Chairman, to make a grant of twenty pounds to Brendon Coombe Hotspur to help them buy a new set of goalposts for the rapidly approaching season, the old set having been sawn up by vandals. That had provided a neat little story for the Clarion - unlike the meandering discussions concerning the granting of a parsimonious twenty pounds.

The reporter had thought for a moment that there might have been a bit of mileage in an item on the agenda marked, 'obscene graffiti written on the walls of the Parish Hall: to determine a course of action.' Unfortunately for the Clarion, the course of action decided upon was to refer the matter to the next meeting of the Parish Hall sub-committee, for them to report to the full council at a later date. So although there could still be a good tale coming out of those proceedings, there would be nothing which would fill the columns of the paper that week. Another protracted discussion followed, concerning the buying of a new typewriter for the part-time clerk, George Miller, who was also the local postmaster. The council accepted that he needed a new one, the old machine being on its last legs, but they were concerned at the price, which was put at around two hundred pounds. It was decided in the end - unanimously this time - to delay a decision until the clerk had had time to contact various office equipment companies and find out just what sort of discount could be had if the council paid cash, and if any of them would be willing to take back the old typewriter in part exchange.

It was at this point that Alan Burton had thrown down his pen. Rarely had there been such a waste of an evening, and a glance at the remaining items on the agenda convinced him that there was nothing still to come which could possibly make his journey, and time, that evening, worthwhile. He looked at his watch, saw the time was past eight thirty and pondered whether or not it was time to call it a night - and go home.

To his surprise, however, the decision was made for him - and, in consequence, his innate curiosity and suspicion was roused.

"Item 7 - report of special meeting of the cemetery sub-committee," read the Council Chairman, Henry Morris. "Mr Miller, will you distribute copies of the report to the members, please."

"Mr Chairman, before the clerk hands around the reports, could I ask that this item be taken in committee?" asked Gordon Long, the sub-committee chairman, an embarrassed look about him. Henry Morris made no attempt to conceal his surprise: "Taken in committee, Mr Long? I don't recall anything to do with the cemetery being taken in committee before. I've always thought that excluding members of the public and press from any aspects of our proceedings is a course we should not lightly take. The grass roots democracy which we represent can only really flourish in the light of public scrutiny - not in the darkness of secrecy. Can you give me the reason why you feel that this item should be taken in committee?" He gazed somewhat imperiously at the chairman of the cemetery sub-committee, rather proud of his stout defence of democracy! "Well, it's a bit difficult really, Mr Chairman," mumbled Gordon Long, now looking furtive rather than embarrassed. "It's just that I feel the interests of the ratepayers would be best served if this report can be discussed in, well, in private, so that - so that we can reach the right decision for the people of this parish."

"I'm still a little unhappy about this, Mr Long," said the chairman, shaking his head.

"I can understand how you feel, Mr Chairman," Long sympathised - rather excessively - "but I do feel that this item would be better taken in committee. Perhaps, Mr Chairman," he added briskly, "you might care to glance at the report first then possibly you'll see what I mean." The chairman looked puzzled, then shrugged his shoulders. "Very well, Mr Long." He took the sheet of paper proffered him by the Clerk, scanned it quickly, laid it down before him, and looked at the expectant faces before him - and none, now, more expectant, and interested, than Alan Burton. He'd been sitting at the back of draughty ante rooms and council chambers for almost twenty years, and he could always pick up the scent of a story wafting through the musty air. And there was certainly one here somewhere, of that he was sure - though whether he could ever really got hold of it was another matter. One thing for sure was that within the space of a couple of minutes his soporific boredom had changed to intense interest.

"Yes, I think possibly this item would best be taken in committee," said the chairman softly. "Do I have a seconder?" Councillor Mrs Jenkins raised her hand to signify her seconding of the motion.

The chairman glanced around at the other members of the council. "Members agree that we take this item in committee?" A series of 'ayes' and nods indicated their assent. Henry Morris gazed toward the back of the room at the two male ratepayers, and the single journalist, present. "Thank you for your attendance, gentlemen, but unfortunately I must ask you to leave the ante room as this item is to be taken in committee."

The three observers got slowly to their feet and noisily trudged from the room, Alan Burton bringing up the rear, his curiosity intense and determined to be satisfied - though he was aware that it could take a while to do that. Martin Mullins would not have a good lead story from this direction for this week's edition, but there were a few columns to come sometime, of that the deputy editor was certain.

As soon as Burton had closed the door behind him, Henry Morris restarted the proceedings. "Perhaps you'll distribute copies of the report, Mr Mullins," he instructed the Clerk, "then we can get down to discussing it - and the figures in it."

"Yes, the figures in it, Mr Chairman," said Gordon Long. "That's the reason I felt it was vital this report be taken in Committee."

"I agree, Mr Long," retorted the Chairman, his face looking almost ashen. "Mind you, I do dislike any aspects of secrecy concerning council business, but I must say that at first glance it would be in nobody's interest for the contents of this report to be made public at present. Still, perhaps you'll take us through it, Mr Long, and explain to us the fearsome figures it seems to contain."

"Certainly, Mr Chairman," said Gordon Long, looking around at his colleagues with an uneasy combination of self importance and apprehension about him. "Firstly, perhaps I ought to remind members of the background to this report."

"Yes - good idea," replied the Chairman. "I expect most of us could do with a recap on it. After all, it's many months since we asked Mr Markwell, the surveyor, to prepare a report on the

'Chapel of Rest'."

"Why did we go to Markwell, Mr Chairman?" asked Councillor Arnold Atkins. "He's not a man I've got any faith in. He surveyed a house I was interested in buying and said it was in excellent condition. I bought it as a result of that report yet just over twelve months after we moved in, my missus went through the floorboards in the front room."

"I'm not surprised seeing the size of his missus," Councillor Sid Bowen muttered to the aged Councillor, Stanley Cowling, sitting slumped down beside him.

"Rotten's a pear it was, Mr Chairman," continued Atkins, becoming more irate by the minute. "I wouldn't have Markwell in any house of mine ever again after that lot. Tried to sue him, but didn't get anywhere - you know how these buggers wriggle out of any responsibility for anything. I told my solicitor to take action but.........."

"Yes, it must have been a most upsetting business, Mr Atkins," interjected Henry Morris quickly - though using a sympathetic tone of voice. It was, he knew, important to stop Arnold Atkins before he really got going. "Still, I don't think this council have ever had any reason to question Mr Markwell's professional abilities."

"Quite so, Mr Chairman," agreed the parish clerk.

"That doesn't altogether answer Mr Atkins' question though, does it Mr Chairman?" pointed out the astute Mrs Jenkins. "He wanted to know why we go to Markwell and Company - and so do I. Speaking personally, I've nothing particular against Mr Markwell - though I have heard one or two stories, not exactly to his credit, especially concerning his private life."

"Really Mrs Jenkins, the surveyor's private life is absolutely nothing to do with this council," the Chairman scolded - quite severely.

"I agree, Mr Chairman," replied the lady, a little contritely, "but I've also heard criticism of his professional abilities - quite apart from Mr Atkins' this evening. It could be though that Mr Markwell is an excellent surveyor. All I'd like to know is why we go to him when there are others in the district we could use. Granted there is none practising in this parish, but there are two other companies providing surveying services in Bowminster. Why do we always go to Markwell and Company and never to either of them?"

The clerk looked puzzled. "Well, simply because we always have, Mr Chairman. We used to go to old Markwell years ago and when he retired, we naturally used the services of his son."

"Old man Markwell didn't retire - he died," rasped Stanley Cowling, not moving one inch from his semi-reclining position. The clerk looked puzzled for a few seconds - as he often did - then nodded his head. "I do believe Mr Cowling is correct, Mr Chairman," he said, a little pompously - as was his wont. "However, with due respect, I feel this is all somewhat irrelevant. Both old Mr Markwell and the present one have generally served this Council well over the years, and I can frankly see no reason to question the judgement of either. Obviously Mr Atkins has had an unsatisfactory personal experience regarding Mr Markwell but I feel that it's only fair for the council to speak as it finds, as the saying goes."

"Yes, I agree, Mr Chairman," said Gordon Long impatiently. "Markwell's always been reasonably efficient to my mind. He certainly did a good job in finding that leak in the parish hall wall a few years back when we called him in because of the fungus growing in the kitchen, so as far as I'm concerned, there's no need to question his conclusions in this report."

"What are his conclusions in this report?" asked Sid Bowen rather irritably.

"Well, Mr Chairman, members have got them in black and white in front of them and, if I'm ever given a chance to, I'll explain them fully," replied Long, tartly.

"Point of order, Mr Chairman."

"Yes, Mr Cowling," said Henry Morris, somewhat wearily.

"Well, it's the state of these reports. I don't know about everybody else, but I can hardly read mine. It's just as well Mr Long is going to go through it. They should be clearer than this, surely," rasped the aged councillor. "Why, we've only recently bought a new photo-copier."

"Actually it's almost ten years since we bought the copier, Mr Chairman, and even then it was second hand," retorted the clerk, sharply. "It's almost had its day, I'm afraid, but I'm willing to soldier on with it at present in order to save the council what would be quite considerable expenditure. The typewriter, however," he added quickly, suddenly remembering the fight he'd made earlier in the meeting to get a new one, "remains absolutely vital. The old one there really has had it."

"So's the photo-copier as far as I can see, Mr Chairman," said councillor Cyril Pellow, chairman of the Finance and General Purposes Committee. "And I would suggest that the council receiving clear photo-copies of various reports and minutes is more important than the parish clerk being able to save a few minutes typing a letter." He glared at the clerk as he said it - no love had been lost between the two since George Miller had put too little in the estimates a couple of years earlier to cover the cost of new play equipment for the children's play area in the park, then deftly passed the buck to Pellow when a group of irate parents called a public meeting over the matter.

"Perhaps we could form a small sub committee to discuss all aspects of office equipment required by the Parish Clerk," suggested Henry Morris, aware that if he didn't take some action then the meeting could meander on until midnight and still not get to the nitty gritty of what Gordon Long was trying to report.

"All right, I'll go along with that, Mr Chairman," agreed Pellow, knowing that as Chairman of Finance he could probably, on a small sub-committee, block any moves to give the Clerk a new typewriter. George Miller was well aware of this. "Mr Chairman, is it really necessary to waste members time with yet another sub-committee," he cried.

"I don't think it'll be a waste of time, Mr Miller," replied the Chairman. "No, I fancy it'll be a good idea. A sub committee like this can really go into what is needed in the office and come up with a list of priorities. I don't suppose we'll be able to afford much on the list, mind you, but at least we'll know what is really needed, and in what sequence."

"The usual members on the sub-committee I assume, Mr Chairman?" asked Cyril Pellow innocently.

"Yes, I think so," replied Morris. "Chairman and vice chairman of the council, and chairman of properties and finance committees. Members agree?"

Members appeared to agree.

"Right - now let's get on with this report. Mr Long, please."

"Thank you, Mr Chairman. As I said just now, perhaps it would be best if I gave members the background, briefly, to this report - though I'm sure many will be aware of what it's all about anyway."

"Carry on, Mr Long," intoned the Chairman.

"Thank you, Mr Chairman," said the ever courteous, and very shrewd, Gordon Long. "Now several years ago, after complaints from the Vicar - and one or two from Harvey Hancock the undertaker - about the deteriorating condition of the Chapel of Rest at the cemetery, we asked Mr Markwell to prepare a report on the defects at the Chapel, and how much it would take to put it right."

"Was that the present Mr Markwell, or his father?" asked Mrs Jenkins, who'd only come onto the council at the last election.

"Oh, the present one," replied Long. "The old chap's been dead these fifteen years or more, whilst the first report, which I'm referring to at present, was brought to us about five years ago. Now, in that report to the council, Markwell said that whilst the condition of the Chapel of Rest was not half as bad as the vicar and the undertaker made out, there were, nonetheless, things which needed doing, especially to the roof; and a certain amount of re-pointing of the stonework was also deemed advisable. Mr Markwell estimated the total cost of the work at not more than a thousand pounds and, as I recall, advised the council to have the work done before the following Winter. As his report was made to us in the early Summer, there was adequate time in which the work could have been done before the short days came upon us, Mr Chairman, but sadly this did not happen. The council in its wisdom decided to shelve the report saying, as I recall, that whilst Markwell's advice would be kept in mind, there was no money, at that time, to put the work in hand."

Arnold Atkins jumped to his feet. "Mr Chairman, I refuse to sit here and listen to Mr Long implying that it was the council's fault that no action was taken," he roared angrily. "As I recall it, most of us were in favour of doing some of the work, if not all, but Mr Long himself talked us out of it. He was chairman of the finance committee at the time and said that we simply could not afford any expenditure on the Chapel of Rest seeing as we'd over spent so heavily on improving the changing rooms up at the recreation field. I've got a good memory, Mr Chairman, and those are the facts - as you, yourself, might well recall."

Gordon Long's face flushed with anger and embarrassment. "Well obviously we couldn't spend money we didn't have, Mr Chairman," he retorted. "But of course we would have had ample funds if we'd not spent a small fortune in refurbishing the playing field changing rooms - which, incidentally, was to the real advantage only of the football club of which Mr Atkins was, and I believe remains, the chairman."

Arnold Atkins scrambled once again to his feet, his face brick red, his eyes bulging from their sockets - as they invariably did when anger was his master. "Mr Chairman, Mr Chairman," he spluttered. "I will not have my integrity questioned in this manner. The improvements to those changing rooms were to the advantage of the entire village; the entire parish in fact - not just the football club. Scores of folk use them, all the year round, not just players in the village club. The cricket club use them through the Summer because the changing rooms in their pavilion don't have running water. The scouts use them for............"

"Yes, yes, quite so, Mr Atkins," soothed Henry Morris. "I'm sure we all accept that the refurbishments made to the changing rooms were to the advantage of the entire parish - and I'm sure Mr Long was in no way questioning your integrity."

"He damned well was, Mr Chairman," retorted Atkins, still looking apoplectic.

"In my opinion he was not, Mr Atkins," ruled the Chairman, severely. "So please let us have no more of this needless argument, gentlemen. The situation is that a previous report of Mr Markwell was not acted upon - five years ago or whatever it was

- and now we have another report from him which Mr Long is about to take us through."

Henry Morris was, generally, mild mannered, but when he had that certain look of annoyance about him, few would venture to argue with the man. Arnold Atkins had more sense, and respect for convention, than to directly confront the Chairman. Yet he was a stubborn, tenacious man, and was determined to have the last word on the matter. "I accept your ruling, Mr Chairman, of course," he said evenly. "However, I would like to point out before we move on, that if it had been deemed essential to have carried out this work on the Chapel of Rest at that time, then the money could quite easily have been raised by levying a half penny rate or by borrowing."

"Mr Chairman, it's never been the policy of this council, except in the most dire emergencies, to raise money either by the levying of a supplementary rate - or charge as it is now - or by borrowing," retorted Long. "There are occasions - albeit very few - when it is necessary to go to the chargepayers by levying an emergency charge, but it would have been difficult to have justified it on that occasion, even though it was important to have carried out the work on the Chapel of Rest - as we realise now. For if we had done the necessary repairs then, we wouldn't be having to face up to this report, with all its wide ranging implications, this evening. Mr Chairman, I submit that........"

Nobody was ever to know what Gordon Long was about to submit, for Henry Morris' patience suddenly snapped: "Mr Long, I ruled some minutes ago that you should proceed to take us through the report which lies in front of us," he snapped. "I trust you will now do so without comment upon things long past - and that includes you as well, Mr Atkins."

"Very well, Mr Chairman," acceded Long, demurely. Arnold Atkins said nothing at all.

"This report, Mr Chairman," continued the chairman of the cemetery sub committee, "was, as I said just now, compiled by Mr Markwell acting upon instructions from this council some months ago. We were concerned about the ever deteriorating state of the Chapel of Rest at the cemetery - as members no doubt remember."

"Get on, Mr Chairman," grunted Sid Bowden, "that isn't the reason and Mr Long knows it. We asked for this report because the vicar and the undertaker kept on moaning about the state of the chapel - as they have for donkeys' years now. I opposed wasting our money on paying Markwell's excessive fees the last time, and, as members might well remember, I opposed it again a few months ago. These reports are a waste of time and money, because they forever tell us to spend money we haven't got on an old relic we should not be maintaining."

"But the chapel is council property, Mr Bowden," reasoned Henry Morris in the most accommodating tone of voice. He knew just how bloody-minded Sid Bowden could be when he got going - and by how much he could lengthen a meeting. "As such, we are obliged to maintain it to a reasonable standard - I'm sure you will agree."

"And it's a listed building," chipped in Councillor Mrs Higgins, who was always well up on such matters.

"Yes, that's a good point, Mrs Higgins," agreed the council chairman. "We shall certainly be in trouble with the conservationists, not to mention the district council, if we let the place fall down."

"If they want the chapel to be maintained in good order, Mr Chairman, then they should foot the bills," persisted Bowden.

"Marvellous it is; this council gets not the slightest benefit from that chapel yet we've got to use our money to maintain it."

"Not our money, Mr Chairman," interjected Stan Cowling, "the chargepayers money."

"All right, I accept that - the chargepayers money," agreed Bowden. "And what good is the place to the chargepayers of this parish, Mr Chairman?" he asked aggressively.

"None, unless they're dead," grunted Arnold Atkins.

"The only people who benefit from that Chapel, Mr Chairman," continued Bowden doggedly, "are the vicar and Harvey Hancock, the undertaker. The vicar holds the occasional funeral service there if he knows hardly anybody is going to turn up, whilst Hancock uses it as his own personal Chapel of Rest which means he doesn't have to provide one of his own, like most undertakers do. They're the two who should be maintaining the chapel, not us."

The parish clerk intervened hastily, "Mr Hancock does pay a rental to this council for the right to use the Chapel of Rest for his - his......"

"His customers I suppose you could call them, Mr Miller," said Henry Morris, with a rare show of humour.

"Quite, Mr Chairman," said the parish clerk, with a sickly smile. George MIller had no sense of humour, at all.

"How much does he pay, Mr Chairman?" asked Arnold Atkins.

"Fifty pounds a year, Mr Chairman," replied the clerk.

"What?" roared Sid Bowden. "Why, that's less than a pound a week, Mr Chairman. That's ridiculous. How long's he been paying that amount?"

George Miller shrugged his shoulders, "I don't know, Mr Chairman. That's always been the amount he's paid during the -

what is it, now, sixteen or seventeen years I've been Clerk to this Council. He pays quarterly."

"I don't believe this, Mr Chairman." Sid Bowden was in full flood now. "Are we being told that Harvey Hancock has been on a rental of one pound a week for more than seventeen years?"

"Well, - yes, that's what I'm saying, Mr Chairman," retorted the clerk. Bowden eyed the clerk belligerently, then lowered his voice. "Are any other undertakers permitted to use the Chapel of Rest, Mr Chairman?" he asked.

"Well, - no, not really, Mr Chairman," replied George Miller, avoiding Bowden's eye. "The Chapel of Rest can be used by other undertakers - which means undertakers from outside the parish seeing as Mr Hancock is the only one within it - when the actual burial service is to be held there, of course. On those occasions, the Chapel of Rest ceases to be that, Mr Chairman, but becomes a chapel in the normal sense, for the vicar to say words over the deceased, and for mourners to attend, and for hymns to be sung and so on. But when it is used in its normal capacity, as a Chapel of Rest for the accommodation of a corpse filled coffin until it is removed to the parish church, or to the United Reform Chapel or whatever, for the full burial service, then Mr Hancock has the exclusive use of the Chapel of Rest."

"For a pound a week," rasped Sid Bowden. "All those years ago when the rent was first fixed, a pound a week would have been peanuts. After all, even then he could never have rented a like building to lay a coffin for a trifling sum like that. But these days a pound a week will hardly cover the council's costs in collecting it."

"Oh, it costs virtually nothing to collect, Mr Chairman," interjected the clerk. "I just send Mr Hancock a quarterly account and usually he sends a cheque by return - though sometimes he calls personally and pays."

"You know what I mean," snapped Bowden. "What I want to know, though, is why his rent has never been increased. The parish clerk is as well aware as any of us - in fact, more aware by virtue of his position - of just how tight finances have been for this council over recent years, yet he's allowed a situation to carry on where a quite prosperous local businessman is paying what is nothing more than a peppercorn rent for a valuable piece of council property."

"Mr Chairman, I resent Councillor Bowden's remarks!" cried George Miller jumping to his feet. "As clerk to this council, I am but a paid employee. I have neither the power nor the right to adjust rents to council tenants. I am but a servant of the council, and act as I am bid. If the Council had told me to put up Mr Hancock's rent, then it would have been done immediately. Of course, if we're to get technical about it, it's something which should have been looked into by the cemetery sub committee. They could, and should, have proposed a new rental for Mr Hancock, and the full council would no doubt have approved it."

"Mr Chairman, I must protest," snapped Gordon Long. "The cemetery sub committee is a hard-working group, but we are an ever changing body as are all sub-committees. At every Annual General Meeting, the composition is changed as the parish clerk well knows. So it's down to him to keep us informed of what's happening and what needs looking into. Even though I'm chairman of the cemetery committee, this is the first time I've ever heard that Harvey Hancock only pays a pound a week in rent. I share Mr Bowden's shock and anger at this ludicrous rental and would ask, Mr Chairman, that this issue be put on the agenda of the next meeting of the cemetery sub committee, when a new and realistic rent can be fixed."

"That sounds an excellent idea, Mr Long," replied the Chairman. "Members agree?" There was universal assent. "See that item is added to the agenda, Mr Miller, will you?"

"Very well, Mr Chairman," replied the parish clerk in clipped tones. He didn't like being a whipping boy for council incompetence, and felt that it was happening increasingly often. And if they were talking about pittance rents, perhaps it was time they talked of the pittance they paid him for listening to their meandering deliberations, and carrying out their, so often, woolly-headed instructions. The time had come for him to seriously think about chucking it all in. If he resigned, then perhaps they'd realise just how much he'd done for them over the years. Still, if he did go, he'd miss the quarterly cheque he drew from the council - inadequate though it most certainly was. But they would push him too far one day, of that he was sure, and it could be that such a day was not that far distant.

"If a new rental's going to be fixed for Harvey Hancock at the next Cemetery meeting, Mr Chairman, then surely we ought to fix a new amount for the vicar as well," said Arnold Atkins. "What does he pay at present?"

The chairman looked at the parish clerk. "What does the vicar pay at present, Mr Miller?" he asked.

"I don't quite follow, Mr Chairman," replied the Clerk. "Where does the vicar come into this?"

"He occasionally uses the Chapel of Rest doesn't he?" retorted Atkins, a little crossly. "That's where he comes in. How much does he pay every time he actually holds a funeral service in our Chapel of Rest - that's all I want to know?"

The clerk's face assumed a puzzled expression - a not rare event. "The vicar pays nothing, Mr Chairman. Why should he?"

"Why should he?" roared Arnold Atkins. "Because he's using council property to make money for himself, that's why he should be paying a fee."

"I don't quite follow, Mr Chairman," commented the clerk, putting on what Stan Cowling always termed, his 'Stan Laurel' face.

"Well, he doesn't plant 'em for nothing," rasped the exasperated Atkins. "Every time he buries somebody, he charges a fee - and that includes those occasions when he holds the service in our Chapel of Rest and not in the parish church. So whenever he uses our property when about his business - because, at the end of the day, that's what it is, his business and his living - he should pay the council a reasonable fee. I'm absolutely dumbfounded he doesn't already do so. This appears to me, Mr Chairman, and I hate to say this - but it appears to me to be another example of incompetence on the part of........"

"Yes, well, I don't think there's any need to get personal, Mr Atkins," interjected Henry Morris before the acerbic Atkins could spit out the name - although everybody knew whose name was on his tongue. "I think this issue should also be added to the agenda of the next cemetery sub committee."

"Very well, Mr Chairman," said the parish clerk with unusual haste, not even giving the Chairman the chance to get the formal approval of the council regarding his suggestion. The quicker deliberations moved on from their present inquisitional style enquiries concerning the undertaker and the vicar, the better for all concerned - especially himself. Henry Morris glanced at the parish clerk, an expression of mild annoyance on his face. He didn't like being hustled in this way, but with the slightest shrug of his shoulders, decided to let the matter go. After all, time was running on and they'd still not got down to the report.

"Now perhaps we can get into this report, ladies and gentlemen," he said briskly. "My glance at it before we went into committee suggests to me that there are financial problems and implications coming our way which will tend to make discussions concerning rents and fees paid by undertakers and vicars just a little irrelevant - though, I would agree that such matters do need discussing and updating as a matter of urgency," he added quickly. "Mr Long, would you take us into the real core of this report - and the reasons why you felt it should be taken in committee."

"Yes, of course, Mr Chairman." Gordon Long gazed, owl like, through his thick glasses, the expression on his face suitably grave. "Perhaps members will ignore the preamble of this report and look at paragraph 6. As I said earlier, Mr Markwell was instructed to prepare this report some months ago following complaints as to the condition of the Chapel of Rest. In paragraph 6, he tells exactly what's wrong with it and I'm sure you'll find it somewhat harrowing reading."

"Get on, it can't be as bad as what he says," snapped Stan Cowling. "That Chapel of Rest was built about a hundred and fifty years ago when they knew how to build these kind of places. It'll be standing there when our grandchildren are dead and gone."

"Not according to this report, Mr Chairman, I'm afraid," opined Gordon Long. "Mr Markwell suggests that if we do not act immediately, there is a very real risk that the Chapel of Rest will deteriorate so much during the next six to twelve months that it will become impossible to use it. In fact, it could even become dangerous to use it. He says that the roof is in such a bad way, it urgently needs replacing, whilst any amount of work needs doing to the windows and general stonework. And he does stress, Mr Chairman, that this work be put in hand virtually right away if long term disaster is to be avoided."

"Twelve thousand pounds!" cried Mrs Higgins, glancing down the single sheet report to the final paragraph at the bottom. "That's what he says it'll cost to put it right. Twelve thousand pounds; where do we get money like that, Mr Chairman?"

"Nowhere, that's the simple answer to that question," snapped Arnold Atkins. "It might as well be twelve million pounds, Mr Chairman. There's no way we can find the sort of money Markwell's talking about here - and there's no way we should even try."

"I feel we have to try, Mr Atkins," replied the chairman. "If we don't, then the Chapel of Rest will simply fall down."

"Let it," rasped Sid Bowden. "If it does, all it'll mean is that the undertaker will have to find fresh premises to lay his coffins - and pay a realistic rental for them - whilst the vicar won't have a council sponsored chapel to hold funeral services in. I reckon, Mr Chairman, that we would do the ratepayers of this parish a service if we let it fall down."

"We can't, Mr Chairman," insisted Mrs Higgins. "As I said earlier, it's a listed building. We'll be in all sorts of trouble from so many groups, including probably the Department of the Environment, if we do nothing."

"Then they can pay for it," growled Bowden.

"Members will probably understand now, Mr Chairman, why I felt this matter should be taken in committee," said Gordon Long with an air of self importance.

"I'm sure nobody disputes the wisdom of it, Mr Long," replied the Chairman rather curtly, seeing Long's comment as being totally superfluous.

"Good God, I should think it does need to be taken in committee, Mr Chairman!'' cried Cyril Pellow. ''If Alan Burton of the Clarion was ever to get hold of this lot, then he'd crucify us.''

''It's not our fault,'' grunted Stan Cowling.

''I'm not saying it is,'' retorted Pellow. ''But if he put in the Clarion that we refused to act on a report five years ago because it was going to cost a thousand pounds, and now it's going to cost twelve, then I reckon we'd be made to look the biggest bunch of incompetent fools that ever sat on the council.''

''And it's elections next May. I don't think there'd be many of us get back on the council if the chargepayers heard a tale like that,'' said Stan Cowling.

''But they must hear such a tale, Mr Chairman,'' pleaded Mrs Higgins. ''There's no way around it. In fact I'm not at all sure it was a wise or necessary move to go into committee.''

''You didn't say that earlier when I suggested we should,'' retorted Gordon Long.

''Well - no, that's true. But I was influenced by yourself and the reaction of the chairman after he'd glanced through the report. I see now though, with hindsight, that I should have voted against it. If it had been discussed in public then we couldn't be accused of trying to cover anything up.''

''But we are trying to cover something up - surely,'' said Pellow.

''We're not covering anything up, Mr Chairman,'' snapped Long, rather crossly. ''At present we're merely discussing this report.''

''Then we're going to do nothing about it,'' persisted Pellow. ''It'll be discussed, then the clerk will be told to put it at the bottom of a file, and at the bottom of a cupboard somewhere. And we'll all hope that the Chapel of Rest doesn't fall down for the foreseeable future."

"Not until after May, anyway," grunted Stan Cowling, once again.

"Why all this insistence that we'll not act on this report, Mr Chairman?" the annoyed Mrs Higgins chipped in. "As I see it, we have to act - we have no option."

"I don't know about having no option, Mr Chairman," retorted Pellow. "The one certainty in my mind is that we have no money. That, simply, is the reason why we will take no action on this report."

"Surely we have a reserve of money put by for emergencies, Mr Chairman," said Mrs Jenkins.

"Well - yes I believe we do, Mrs Jenkins. That is so, Mr Miller, isn't it?"

"Quite right, Mr Chairman," replied the parish clerk. "I always put a sum of money in the estimates to take care of any emergencies which might crop up regarding council property throughout the year."

"How much?" asked Stan Cowling.

"Five hundred pounds, Mr Chairman," replied Miller, briskly.

"Five hundred quid? That'll hardly settle Markwell's bill, let alone anything else," rasped Cyril Pellow. "The situation is as I said a moment ago - we have no money."

"We can raise some," persisted Mrs Higgins.

"How?" asked Pellow.

"We can levy a charge. Or perhaps borrow the money. There must be some way we can raise it." Mrs Higgins was a very persistent woman.

"How large a supplementary charge would we have to levy to raise twelve thousand pounds?" asked Henry Morris of the clerk. George Miller looked nonplussed for a few seconds, then scribbled for a brief period on a pad in front of him. "We might just be able to raise enough on a fourpenny one, Mr Chairman," he retorted, dropping his pen noisily onto his desk as he spoke. Stan Cowling's mouth dropped open like a trapdoor. "A four penny charge," he exclaimed. "If we try levying a four penny charge then I'm damned sure none of us'll be re-elected next May."

"Quite so," agreed Cyril Pellow. "There's no way we can levy a supplementary charge of that size, Mr Chairman. As I said just now, we must take no action on this report. File it and forget it, that's what I say."

"But the place could collapse - possibly even kill somebody." Mrs Higgins was not to be defeated that easily.

"If it collapses on somebody, Mr Chairman, the chances are he'll already be dead," grunted Stan Cowling.

"But we cannot have the place collapsing; it's-it's a listed building as I said just now."

"Typical of the district council and the ministry, and so on, that is, Mr Chairman. They list a building as being of special architectural interest, or historic interest or some old nonsense, tell parish councils like us we've got to preserve them and such like, then don't give you a brass farthing to do it with," grumbled Arnold Atkins. "No, it's best for the chargepayers of this parish that we take no action whatsoever; I agree entirely with Mr Pellow on that point."

"There are ways of getting a grant towards doing this work, Mr Chairman, seeing as it's a listed building," chipped in the clerk, trying to sound helpful.

"The speed they pay out these grants, Mr Chairman," said Sid Bowden, "the place'll be a pile of rubble long before we ever see a penny of it. And even then, we would only get a small percentage of the total cost - isn't that right?" Both his tone of voice and the expression on his face were somewhat belligerent as he turned his gaze upon the parish clerk, whom he'd long considered to be an incompetent idiot.

"Well, yes," agreed the clerk, in a subdued voice. "These things do tend to take some considerable time and we would only get a percentage of the total cost, Mr Chairman."

"What size percentage?" asked Mrs Higgins.

"Well, I'm afraid I don't really know off hand, Mr Chairman," muttered the clerk, in even more subdued tones.

"If he doesn't know something as important as that, then the parish clerk's not doing his job correctly, Mr Chairman," snapped Cyril Pellow, never slow to have a dig at the hapless Miller.

"Mr Chairman, I resent that," retorted the clerk. "I can't be expected to know everything."

"Perhaps not," retorted Pellow, "but I would suggest that the clerk, knowing the financial implications of the Chapel of Rest report to this Council, should have come to this meeting with all details of how we could apply for any grants we'd be entitled to, Mr Chairman. The fact that it's unlikely we would pursue this path is irrelevant." Stan Cowling leant forward in his seat and opened his mouth to, probably, voice support for Pellow, but the Chairman stilled him with a wave of his hand. George Miller didn't altogether deserve it, because Cyril Pellow was certainly correct, but Henry Morris felt obliged, as Chairman, to come to his clerk's aid.

"I think we've had sufficient of this, Mr Pellow," he said in his customarily calm way. "It could be that the parish clerk might have over-looked information regarding grants we might have taken up, but even if he had, it's extremely unlikely we'd have availed ourselves of such a grant. It would almost certainly take far too long and produce far too little - as we said just now. So let's drop this - this interrogation - and try to reach a decision as to what we are going to do concerning this report."

"Can we borrow the money?" asked Mrs Higgins, still not prepared to give up her fight to have something positive done towards restoring the Chapel of Rest.

"There's no way we can borrow any more money, Mr Chairman," chimed in the clerk quickly. "This council already owes more money than is wise, to be frank. The buying of the new tractor last year is the cause, of course; we had to borrow quite heavily to purchase it. I felt it was the wrong move at the time, and I feel the same way now; there was no reason why we had to have our own tractor. We could have continued to hire one on a daily basis from Mr Billings at Oakfield Farm as we'd done, without any problems, for years. But I wasn't listened to, Mr Chairman, I'm afraid, and as a result, we're in debt. I have to say......."

"Mr Miller, you made your feelings felt regarding this matter when it was discussed last year. Rightly or wrongly the decision was still made to purchase a tractor, and to borrow money to do so. That's an end to it, Mr Miller," admonished the Chairman. "I want to hear nothing more about it."

"Very well, Mr Chairman," replied the Clerk huffily.

"That seems to settle it then, Mr Chairman," said Gordon Long. "We daren't try to raise the money to renovate the Chapel of Rest through the rates, and we can't borrow. So the only thing we can do is to close it down."

"But we can't just do that. We can't stand by and leave it to eventually fall apart," pleaded Mrs Higgins. "After all, it's a listed building."

"There's no need to close the Chapel, Mr Chairman," said

Arnold Atkins. "All we need to do is to get Harvey Hancock paying a realistic rental, and the vicar paying a fee every time he holds a funeral service there, and carry on as before."

"But Mr Chairman, we can't carry on as before," retorted Gordon Long, exasperation in his voice. "That's what the report is telling us. Twelve thousand pounds is needed to put the Chapel of Rest into a reasonable state of repair. Sadly we don't have that kind of money, we can't raise it through an extra charge, and we can't borrow it. So the only thing we can do is to close the place down - as I've just said."

"And be made to look a bunch of incompetents, Mr Chairman." Arnold Atkins was on his feet again. "Just imagine how the Clarion will go to town on us. A council who five years ago instructed their surveyor to prepare a report on the Chapel of Rest then refuse to act on his findings because they're not willing to find the thousand pounds needed to carry out his recommendations. Then five year later, they pay the same surveyor another princely fee to prepare a similar report on the same Chapel of Rest. In this one, the surveyor tells the Council to do the same things as he did five years earlier but, due to the fact that all the defects have got worse, plus the ravages of inflation, the cost will now be twelve thousand pounds. And the council don't act on this report either - simply because there's no way they can raise the money needed to carry out the recommendation. Instead, the council closes the Chapel of Rest which will mean, probably, that folk who were born, bred and lived all their lives in this parish, will probably be carted off to lie in a Chapel of Rest in Bowminster before being brought back here to be buried. Mr Chairman, Alan Burton's pen will cut us all up into little pieces - and we'll be fed to the ratepayers like bread to ducks. Councillor Cowling remarked a little earlier that there wouldn't be many of us returned at the elections next May, if the ratepayers heard a tale the like of which I've just told - and he's right. And let's be honest, we wouldn't deserve to be re-elected. As it is now, I'm not sure any of us deserve to get on the council again, the way we've wasted time and money on this Chapel of Rest over the years.''

"So what is it you're saying exactly, Mr Atkins?"

"I'm saying this, Mr Chairman. I believe the best and wisest course now is for the council to carry on as if the report was never written. For sure we don't have the money to do anything about it, so it's best to ignore it altogether. We get Hancock and the Vicar to pay realistically for using the chapel - which'll bring in a little more income to the council - and we carry on as before. It seems to me the only sensible thing to do. For if we just carry on then there's no real chance of any bad publicity. I would remind members we're in committee here, so no news of this report should go beyond this room. In fact, there's no real need for anybody to even know this report exists."

"Mr Atkins, people are bound to know the report exists," pointed out the chairman. "Possibly more important, Alan Burton knows it exists. It is, if you care to glance at your agenda, written there for all to see. In fact, as I recall, I read out the item before Mr Long proposed we go into committee. Therefore I fancy it's a bit late to try and pretend the report does not exist."

Arnold Atkins glanced at his agenda. "With respect, Mr Chairman, all it says on the agenda is, 'item 7 - report of special meeting of cemetery sub-committee' - and that's what you read out. That sentence doesn't tell anything. Certainly it doesn't tell anybody that there was anything contentious to discuss, like this report on the Chapel of Rest. I remember last year there was a special meeting of the sub-committee to discuss the cleaning of some of the older gravestones that had got green and slimy over the years. Nothing exactly earth shattering about that, Mr Chairman. So there's no reason why anybody who's even remotely interested should not think that this meeting was about something equally unimportant." An expression of curiosity fluttered across his face.

"As a matter of interest, Mr Chairman, who exactly attended the special cemetery sub-committee meeting that discussed this report?" he asked.

"Well, in actual fact, nobody did, Mr Chairman," replied Gordon Long, with a somewhat bleak smile. "There seemed little point in the sub-committee discussing an important matter such as this when it obviously needed comprehensive discussion by the full council. Anyway, there are only three members on the sub-committee, and I knew the other two - yourself Mr Chairman, who was away on holiday, and Councillor Shaw, who was, and still is, indisposed - would probably not be available for a meeting, until the full council met. So I thought it best - when receiving the report from the parish clerk - as chairman of the sub-committee, to bring it directly to the council for discussion. The formal entry on the agenda regarding report of special meeting of the cemetery sub-committee was only put there to keep our procedures in accordance with standing orders."

"Fair enough," said Atkins. "So we know that the only people, except for Markwell and his staff, who know the report exists, are those in this room at present. I feel, Mr Chairman, that is the way it should remain. So I formally move that this council takes no action on the report, and that the contents of the report be not divulged to anybody not present in this ante room at this precise moment."

"I second that, Mr Chairman," said Stan Cowling.

"Just a minute, Mr Chairman, it's surely not that simple." There was a pained expression on Gordon Long's face. "This report pointed out several worrying structural defects at the Chapel of Rest, most serious of them being the state of the roof which, according to Mr Markwell, could collapse at almost any time. Mr Chairman we simply cannot ignore a report of this kind. If we cannot afford to do the necessary work - and I accept we cannot at present - then the Chapel of Rest will have to be closed, and we will have to accept any criticism which comes our way. I cannot be party to a pretence that the report does not exist."

"Stuff and nonsense, Mr Chairman," rasped Sid Bowden. "Every council of every size throughout the country suppresses reports now and again. It's all part of democracy at work. And governments - well they do it all the time. 'Not in the public interest', they say when covering something up. Well, it's not in the interests of the public of this parish that they be told the contents of this report. That's what Councillor Atkins has been saying, and I agree with him. Where ignorance is bliss, as the saying goes."

"But Mr Long's point is surely the relevant one, Mr Chairman," insisted Mrs Higgins. "The Chapel of Rest, according to the report, is dangerous. Therefore it's dangerous to allow members of the public to enter it. I would agree with him that, in the short term, we close it, then take every possible step to raise sufficient funds to carry out the repairs. I would remind members that the Chapel of Rest is not just any old piece of council property - it's a listed building and part of our heritage. We have both a legal and moral duty to restore it as soon as possible."

"Get on, Mr Chairman, it doesn't need 'restoring' as Mrs

Higgins puts it," said Stan Cowling. "There's nothing wrong with the place. That Chapel of Rest was there long before any of us were ever thought of and it'll be there, in good order, long after our grand children have passed on."

"Not according to Mr Markwell's report," retorted Mrs Higgins.

"Get on, I don't take any notice of Markwell," replied Cowling. "He's like all these surveyors, and architects and such like, he's got to justify his fat fee. I dare say the Chapel of Rest could do with a bit of titivating, but, structurally, I'm willing to bet the place is as sound as a bell."

"It seems to me, ladies and gentlemen, that we've had a very full and frank discussion of this matter," intervened the Chairman quickly, aware that if he didn't take some sort of action the discussion could drag on half the night, with nothing fresh contributed.

"I feel it's time to put the issue to the vote. It's been proposed by Councillor Atkins, and seconded by Councillor Cowling, that no action be taken on the report prepared by Markwell and Company concerning the present condition of the Chapel of Rest at the Cemetery, and, furthermore, that the contents of the report remain the knowledge solely of those present in this ante room at present. All those in favour, please show." He counted the votes along with the parish clerk.

"Five in favour," he said.

"Six, surely, Mr Chairman," stated Miller.

"I don't think so, Mr Miller. Still, perhaps members would show again. All those in favour?"

The Chairman and the Clerk counted once again.

"There, five," said Henry Morris.

"Do you know, I made it six again, Mr Chairman"

"Perhaps you'd state the names of the six. That's the only way to get this right."

"Certainly, Mr Chairman. Councillors Atkins, Cowling, Bowden, Pellow, Mrs Jenkins and Mrs Higgins."

"I've not voted for the motion, Mr Chairman!" cried out an angry Mrs Higgins. "I should have thought by now that I had made my opposition to this motion more than apparent. This is the most scandalous action this council has ever considered taking during the seven years I've been on it."

"But you put your arm up just now when the vote was held," wailed George Miller.

"I did not, Mr Chairman. I was merely rearranging my hair, some of which had fallen down over my right ear."

"Women," muttered Stan Cowling, shaking his head sadly.

"Well, how was I supposed to know that, Mr Chairman," snapped the clerk. "It looked to me that....."

"I realised it, Mr Miller," interjected the Chairman. "In fact, it was clear to me that Mrs Higgins was not voting in favour of the motion. As she said, after the debate we've just had, it's obvious that she never could. So - there are five in favour of the motion. All those against?"

The chairman cast his eyes over his council. "Two," he said firmly.

"Yes - two," said the clerk, authoritatively. "Mr Long and Mrs Higgins. Other members, I assume, including yourself, Mr Chairman, are abstaining."

"It would appear that way, Mr Miller," agreed the chairman. "Anyway, the motion is carried. No action will be taken on this report; it will be filed and will not be spoken of outside this room. Will somebody please move 'open committee', then we can deal with the final two items on the agenda - and get away home."

XXXXXXXXXXXX

Councillor Stan Cowling's forecast that the Chapel of Rest would 'be there, in good order, long after our grandchildren have passed on' turned out to be somewhat inaccurate. For six weeks exactly after the meeting which decided the report should be shelved, and its contents not divulged, the storm broke - both literally and metaphorically.

The wind was rising towards gale force as Alan Burton made his way from his car to the bar of the 'Sportsman's Inn', a pub on the edge of Bowminster. When he left two hours later, the wind was shrieking like a demented demon, though Burton didn't really notice it; his mind was trying to assess how best to handle the exceedingly interesting news he'd just been given. It had certainly been a profitable session at the bar, he mused, as he clambered into his car, the, by now, heavy rain slanting searchingly into, and through, his lightweight suit. He'd a feeling that if he dug around just a bit the following day, then he could well have a splendid lead story for the weekly edition of the Clarion due out, as always, on Friday. During the time since he'd been asked to leave the meeting of the Brendon Coombe Parish Council, Burton had asked a few questions to a few folk here and there but had made little headway as to what the report contained and what action the council had taken on it. He had learnt though, that Markwell and Company had prepared the report, and had tried the direct approach of asking Markwell himself what the report contained. The surveyor, naturally, pointed out that the report was confidential and could only be made public by the council. Burton went through the motions of contacting the Parish Clerk of Brendon Coombe Parish Council, then the chairman, then, finally, the chairman of the sub committee and got nothing out of any of them - as he'd expected. He would have pursued the matter with his customary zeal - as he was convinced that the council was behaving, at best, deviously, at worst, scurrilously - but the Clarion had run into a rich menu of good stories during recent weeks and he had been so busy filling columns with the local headline making news which was snapping at his heels, that he'd had no real time to probe for the story which, his instinct told him, very much surrounded the report concerning some aspect of Brendon Coombe's cemetery.

That evening though, as he'd lent against the public bar of the Sportsman's, he'd got into conversation with a young fellow whom he only knew vaguely by sight. It transpired, however, that the young man was a trainee surveyor with Markwell, a factor which made him a most interesting drinking companion indeed as far as Alan Burton was concerned - and one to be cultivated. So he saw that the young surveyor's glass was not allowed to remain empty, and was rewarded by an ever more voluble and careless tongue, one, which under subtle questioning from Burton, told him the full contents, and the full significance, of the report compiled by Markwell's, on the Chapel of Rest in Brendon Coombe Churchyard.

"The place could collapse like a house of cards at any time," concluded the slightly tipsy trainee surveyor, with a touch of exaggeration. Those words were very much in Burton's mind as he started up his car and wended his way home through the dark, wet, stormy night. The next morning he would delve and dig amongst the councillors of Brendon Coombe until he had his news item - and it would most certainly be a lead story.

Alan Burton, that night, could not know that the following

morning his story would be there, strewn around Brendon Coombe Cemetery. When he arrived at the Clarion's offices, he made a pot of tea, as usual, and took a cup out to the front office where sat the ancient Beryl a lady who'd been with the paper apparently since the dawn of history, and, virtually, always at the reception desk.

As the deputy editor dropped the cup of tea onto her desk, the main door, leading into the street, opened and a woman came in. "Morning," she said brightly, "I've come to collect the photo I ordered a couple of weeks ago - the one of Brendon Coombe Church Sunday School outing. Mrs Wooley's the name."

At the mention of Brendon Coombe, Alan Burton took some interest in the proceedings.

"Morning, Mrs Wooley," he said affably. "How're things at Brendon Coombe?"

"Well, not too good today," she replied, a serious expression on her face. "The terrible wind through the night has blown the roof off the Chapel of Rest." Burton was stunned - and excited. "Are you sure?" he asked abruptly.

"Oh yes," she replied, "the postman told me first of all, then I saw it myself as I walked past the cemetery to catch the bus. Not all the roof's come off, but about half has gone, with slates and wood and such like scattered all over the cemetery. It's a shame, isn't it? Hundreds of years old that Chapel of Rest, you know."

"It is a shame - it is indeed," agreed Burton, with almost manic glee. He spun on his heels and almost ran to his tiny office at the rear of the building. He had his lead story all right - and he wouldn't have to dig and delve. Yet he needed a quote or two to toss into the columns to give them extra spice. So he phoned Henry Morris, Chairman of Brendon Coombe Parish

Council. Sadly, according to Mrs Morris, her husband was not at home; in fact, he would not be back until late that evening. A likely tale he thought to himself as he dropped the phone onto the receiver. Next he tried George Miller, the parish clerk. He had no trouble getting hold of the man, but it did him little good. "No comment," said the clerk when asked what the council were going to do about the roofless Chapel of Rest - and why they had not acted on the surveyor's report. "I'm merely an employee of the council, and do no more, nor less, than what I am told to do by them. The chairman's the one."

"I've already tried to speak to him," replied Burton, "but he's away until late tonight - according to his wife."

"Then you should speak to the chairman of the cemetery sub-committee, Gordon Long," snapped the parish clerk before putting down the phone.

So Alan Burton did as he suggested, and telephoned Gordon Long. The sub-committee chairman answered the phone himself - mainly because he appeared to be just about the only person in Brendon Coombe Parish not to have heard about the disaster which had struck the Chapel of Rest.

The news shocked him immensely, a fact made apparent by the faltering nature of his voice over the phone. So with his defences in disarray, Alan Burton fired at him the question which was central to his entire projected front page spread.

"Mr Long," he said sternly, "would you not accept that the council has acted very badly in this matter and that it is down to council incompetence and deceit that the Chapel of Rest - which is, I believe, a listed building - is now largely wrecked?"

"No, no, no. It's not the council's fault at all," stuttered Long, well aware that although he felt the report should have been made public and the Chapel of Rest closed, going along with the majority decision of the council made him as much responsible - and vulnerable - as all the other members.

"Then whose fault is it?" persisted the deputy editor.

"Well - well, I suppose, when you get down to it," spluttered the chairman of the cemetery sub-committee. "It's - well, really, nothing more or less than - well, simply an act of God."

# THE TWINNING

Basil Parfitt banged his gavel, and called for order. They were a bit boisterous tonight, he thought, but he'd known them worse. And they had at least moved along at a reasonable pace. That, of course, was largely due to the fact that Denzil Dillow wasn't there. He'd gone down with the 'flu that very morning and, although at the beginning of the meeting Parfitt had wished him a speedy recovery, there was probably nobody in the chamber who was sorry Denzil was absent. For with his constant points of order, his frequent referrals to standing orders and his remarkable ability to make even the most simple issue complicated, he could add an hour to the length of any meeting.

Basil glanced at his watch, then down at the agenda. Only one more item, which shouldn't take long, then he'd be away home - hopefully just in time for the western on TV.

"Item 8 - Any other business," he droned. "I believe Mr Wilson, you've got something you wish to bring before the council."

"Yes, thank you Mr Mayor." Ken Wilson was a tall, well-dressed man, who carried a certain amount of authority with some members of the council by virtue of his impressive bearing. "It concerns a recent holiday I had in France, Mr Mayor. We stayed in a town in Southern Brittany called Guipapont and had a wonderful time there. It's a delightful place, clean, prosperous, and the people are extremely friendly and courteous."

"He'll be showing us his holiday slides next," muttered Councillor Dick Conway to his elderly 'neighbour', Councillor Jim Bennett - who didn't hear him for the simple reason he was in the midst of one of his occasional dozes.

"The town, Mr Mayor, is of similar size to ours - though probably a touch bigger - and, also, like ours, it has a mixture of light industry side by side with an important cattle market and a number of agricultural merchants. Also, near the town, there are............"

"Mr Mayor," thundered Councillor Roland Smith. "I didn't come along here tonight to listen to Mr Wilson's holiday experiences, pleasant though they might well be. So he had a nice holiday in France; well me and my missus had quite a nice one in London - except we were robbed left, right and centre with the prices up there - but I don't intend to waste the valuable time of this council giving a detailed description of it. Mr Mayor, I move next business."

"I think your proposal's a little premature, Mr Smith," replied the Mayor, rather gently. "After all, Mr Wilson's not really got to the point he wishes to raise, yet. However, I would concede that your statement, Mr Wilson, does seem to be rambling on, somewhat; I'm sure we'd all be obliged if you would get to the point." He gave Ken Wilson a somewhat old-fashioned look as he spoke the words.

"I was about to, Mr Mayor," he retorted in his rather imperious fashion, "and would have done so already if I'd not been interrupted by Councillor Smith."

"Saucy bugger," muttered Roland Smith.

"The point of my description of the town of Guipapont, Mr Mayor, is merely to paint a rough picture of the place in the minds of members of the council, for it's important that everyone here has some idea of the kind of town which it is. You see....."

"He's at it again, Mr Mayor!" roared Smith, jumping to his feet with unusual alacrity. "Tell him to get on with it or we'll be here all night."

"I don't need you to instruct me on how to chair this meeting, Mr Smith, thank you very much," retorted the Mayor, rare acidity in his tone. "Still," he continued, shifting his gaze to Ken Wilson, "I trust you will not beat about the bush any longer."

"I wasn't aware, Mr Mayor, that I was beating about the bush at all," retorted Wilson, huffily. "It's not my style to procrastinate and it never has been. However, I feel it's important for members of the council to be aware of the background to the idea I wish to put forward. You see, whilst I was in......"

"Mr Mayor, I've had enough of this," stormed Roland Smith, his face as red as a pillar box. "If Mr Wilson doesn't state exactly what his proposition is, then I shall walk out of this meeting and go home." There had been little love lost between Smith and Wilson, since Ken had publicly criticised Roland's handling, as chairman of the finance committee, of a debate on whether or not to give a grant to the local amateur dramatic society. As Wilson was, and remained, a staunch member of the society, Smith's description of the amateur actions as a 'bunch who should be doing something better with their time', offended him deeply. The chairman's stubborn resistance to the paying of a grant, and his subsequent use of his casting vote to prevent it, created a gulf between the two men which would never be bridged - largely because neither would ever seek to bridge it.

"Mr Smith," replied the Mayor, his voice a little softer than previously, "you're at liberty to leave this meeting, or stay, as you see fit. I, however, will conduct the meeting and decide when a proposition is due. Having said this, I think it time, Mr Wilson, for you to state exactly what you wish to bring before this council. Should you fail to do so, then I shall formally move 'next business' from the chair. Do I make myself clear?"

"Perfectly, Mr Mayor," replied Wilson, evenly, "and I shall, of course, abide by your ruling. With that in mind, I would like to bring before the council, for their consideration, the idea that we might form a twinning link with the town of Guipapont. The reason why I took a couple of minutes actually getting to the point, Mr Mayor, was simply because I felt the council would like some background information regarding the type of town Guipapont is, its size and so on. No doubt councillors will want to know quite a bit more about the place, and I am, of course, very willing to provide such information. However, I felt, because of impatience by certain members of the council who seem unable to lift their minds above the parochial" - he glared at Roland Smith as he said the words - "and because of your ruling, Mr Mayor, that I should put forward the suggestion immediately."

"Point of order, Mr Mayor!" cried Councillor Mrs Harper in her high-pitched way. "Yes, Mrs Harper," replied the Mayor, a tone of weariness about his voice. He might have known that Vera Harper would interrupt somewhere along the line.

"It's just that I wouldn't have thought that the question of twinning was one for this council to discuss, Mr Mayor; I really don't see it as being a council matter."

"Of course, it's a council matter, Mr Mayor,"rasped Councillor Sam Simmonds, impatiently. "I mean, if we don't discuss it, who's going to - Toc H?"

"Yes, obviously it has to be a council matter," agreed the Mayor. "That's if we're talking about an official twinning, of course. Any organisation is at liberty to arrange their own exchange with people of like interests in foreign countries on their own initiative. I know that the football club did this a few years back when they went to Italy for a week. I think they played a few games there and made a lot of good contacts. Then, the following year, the football club of the Italian town visited here. Mind you it doesn't seem to have continued. I've heard of no further exchanges between the two clubs since."

"I'm not surprised, Mr Mayor," rasped Roland Smith, "they were a shocking lot those Italians when they visited here - filthiest footballers I ever saw. In fact one of them broke our centre forward's leg - dirty devil. And off the football field all they did was to drink the pubs dry and chase women."

"Caught one or two as well from what I heard," interjected Councillor Monty Bell.

"Too damned right," agreed Smith. "We don't want them back again, Mr Mayor - nor any others like them either."

"I seem to remember there was a bit of trouble when they were here," agreed Basil Parfitt, "but I'm sure that this was not necessarily a good example of twinning, Mr Smith."

"Of course it wasn't, Mr Mayor," snorted Ken Wilson. "In fact this wasn't really twinning at all; this was merely an exchange between the football clubs of two towns in two separate countries. Nothing wrong with that, of course; in fact such exchanges are a part of twinning. But an official twinning, which is what I'm talking about, is the joining together of two towns at the very top - meaning at council and civic level - and from that other exchanges and associations arise. So if we twin officially with Guipapont, then we sign a twinning charter, we have official twinning visits and everything springs from that. There would be exchanges of school children, sports clubs, probably police and firemen, perhaps Rotary clubs and folk dance clubs and so on. I do believe that such an official link could only bring advantages to the people of this town, Mr Mayor."

"Aren't we twinned with somebody already, Mr Mayor?" asked Jim Bennett, who had been woken from his doze by Roland Smith's tirade a few minutes earlier.

"Not that I know of, Mr Bennett."

"I could have sworn we were twinned with some town in France," continued the aged councillor, doggedly. "Surely we are. Didn't the town's British Legion Club make an official visit?"

The Mayor's face looked blank, as did those of all the other members of the Council. The town clerk, Bernard Dalton, came to the rescue.

"I think, Mr Mayor, that Councillor Bennett is referring to the visit by members of the local Royal British Legion to the battlefields and war graves of Normandy," he said in his customary quiet, respectful, yet efficient manner. "About two years ago that was, Mr Mayor. It was a private visit, of course, nothing to do with any twinning."

"Yes, I remember it now," agreed the Mayor. "That's the explanation, Mr Bennet. No twinning involved there."

Jim Bennett refused to give in. "But the Morris Dancers went as well. I remember that because my nephew's one of them. As I recall, they had to come home early when their chairman, poor old Frank Hammond, dropped dead, in the middle of a dance. Heart. Remember it well, Mr Mayor. That was something to do with twinning, surely?"

Again the Mayor and the members were at a loss - and once more the town clerk stepped into the breach.

"I do believe, Mr Mayor, that there was a visit of the local morris dancers to Holland to take part in a folk dance festival. That again was probably about two years ago - or it might have been a little longer. As Mr Bennett says, Mr Hammond died during the visit - I certainly remember that. Still, it wasn't anything to do with a twinning, of course."

"Can't understand it," persisted Bennett. "I could have sworn we were twinned with somebody, somewhere. Perhaps the clerk can look back through the minutes to see if we are."

"Surely we can't be twinned with somebody and not know it, Mr Mayor," said Councillor Miss Dorothy Parsons, a touch of exasperation in her voice.

"Most unlikely, I would say," agreed the Mayor, urbanely.

"Still, assuming we're not twinned with anyone, it's time we were," continued Dorothy Parsons. "Everybody else seems to be. It's virtually impossible to drive into a city, town or even village now without passing signs giving the name of the place and who they're twinned with. In fact, some places are twinned with two or three overseas towns."

"Exactly, Mr Mayor," chimed in Ken Wilson. "Miss Parsons is right. Some towns and, indeed, villages, much smaller than ours, are twinned with more than one continental place of usually similar size. It is most unusual in this day and age for any town as large as ours not to be twinned with somebody."

"I can't say that I feel deprived in any way that we're not twinned with anybody," rasped Roland Smith. "In fact, I'm pleased we're not if truth be told. Contacts with foreign countries - especially European ones - have never brought any benefits to this country at all. We're an island race, Mr Mayor, and should remember that. The good Lord in his infinite wisdom surrounded us with water to set us aside from other nations; he didn't mean us to fraternise with people on the Continent and such like. Our strength has always lain in our isolation and that should never be forgotten. It's sadly significant, Mr Mayor, that since this twinning nonsense has taken hold throughout the country during the past thirty years or so, this country has gone downhill faster than a horse can gallop. I give fair warning, Mr Mayor, that I shall oppose any move towards officially twinning this town with the Frogs - or anybody else for that matter - with all the energy I can muster. And I'll go so far as to say that should this council decide to have an official twinning, then I shall resign - after serving this town in this chamber for over twenty years. I won't be part of any council who betray the interests of the ratepayers of this town."

As Roland Smith's ample rear hit his seat, the full significance of what he had said overwhelmed him. Where had resignation come from? He'd not had anything like that in mind when he'd stood up to speak. It was that fool Wilson - he was to blame. There was something about the fellow that always got him, Roland, angry. And now his wrath had got him into a fine mess. He shuddered at the thought he might have to resign - and over something so silly. Of course there'd been a few times during his twenty years when he'd threatened resignation, but that had been purely for effect. He'd been well aware then that his bluff wouldn't be called. He wasn't so sure now, though. The council had changed over the years. So many of the old, solid, reliable stalwarts had died, retired or been defeated at elections. There was a sizeable gathering in the chamber of the new breed - those ambitious men and women who wanted "to do things," change the town, squander money, clutter up agendas with resolutions and such like. Several of the "old school" remained, of course, but would they be enough to put a stop to this twinning nonsense? Roland Smith pulled a handkerchief from his trouser pocket and mopped a brow beaded with sweat, despite the coolness of the evening. "I'm afraid, Mr Mayor, that I have to class Councillor Smith's outburst as the rantings of a dinosaur," said Ken Wilson in his smooth, superior kind of way. "I had hoped that such nationalistic, indeed, chauvinistic nonsense, had died long ago, but it would seem I'm wrong. All I can say is that Mr Smith's type of attitude and approach has served this country ill over the years. In fact, I'll go further and suggest that his type of ostrich-like refusal to observe, and learn, from the great strides forward made by so many of our European partners is what has held this country back; for sadly, there are still too many like him in this country. Granted their numbers are getting less, but those of opinions and attitudes similar to Mr Smith are still very prevalent in all aspects of life throughout this land. 'Little Englanders,' is what, I believe, some call them. I would call them small minded, bigoted people totally lacking in vision."

"Just a minute, Mr Mayor!" roared Councillor Graham Phillips - a generally quiet member of the council but one who was always quick to defend a principle or a fellow councillor whom he thought unfairly attacked - jumping to his feet. "That's a scurrilous attack by Mr Wilson. Everyone's allowed to express their opinion in this chamber and that's all Mr Smith's been doing. And I would remind Mr Wilson, and all other members of the council that Councillor Smith with his long years of distinguished war service had more right than most to express opinions about the direction in which the nation appears to be going. And also the right to expect some sort of protection from Mr Wilson's shameful personal attack."

Roland Smith gazed at Phillips, an expression of deep gratitude flitting across his face. Good old Graham, he thought; one of the best - and straight as a die. He'd liked the bit about 'distinguished war service', too. He'd never really considered himself to have had a particularly 'distinguished war service', but then, Graham Phillips was a perceptive man, so could well have been right. It was true he'd never actually left British shores during the hostilities and had only risen to the rank of corporal in the catering corps, but who was to say that he had not performed his duties with distinction and dedication? No, Councillor Phillips could well be right.

"I do tend to agree with you to a certain extent, Mr Phillips," said the Mayor. "Mr Wilson" - he glared at the erring councillor as he spoke his name - "I do feel that your attack on Mr Smith was rather strong and, indeed, unnecessary. He was only expressing a view as is his privilege, so I hope that you refrain from such personal attacks in future."

Ken Wilson got to his feet. "Mr Mayor, if I've offended you, then I apologise," he intoned, not the slightest note of contrition in his voice. "I certainly intended no offence to anyone, but I do feel most strongly upon this matter of twinning - and I feel a certain obligation to the people of this town to try to ensure that out-moded ideas and prejudices do not stand in the way of their taking a full part in the building of bridges between this country and Europe which is going ahead with such speed, and success, in so many other towns throughout our land."

Dorothy Parsons caught the Mayor's eye and got to her feet. "Mr Mayor," she said, "It's all very well us talking about twinning with this French town - Guip - Guip - Guiplonk....."

"Guipapont," corrected Wilson.

"Well, that's what I said, more or less," snapped the somewhat irascible Miss Parsons. "What I'm getting at, Mr Mayor, is simply this - we're talking about twinning with this French town, but how do we know they want to twin with us!"

"Oh, but they do, they do!" cried Wilson. "That's the whole point of me bringing up the subject, Mr Mayor. They are very keen to establish a twinning link with a town in England. I found this out when I had a chat with the Mayor of Guipapont, Monsieur Darleau. I had a most pleasant talk with him one afternoon, Mr Mayor, in his office in the town hall at Guipapont. A most charming and courteous man, he made me feel very welcome. Certainly I was glad I went round to his office to introduce myself. I felt I should, Mr Mayor, as a member of this council. I felt it was most certainly the courteous thing to do."

"He would," muttered Dick Conway, sarcastically, to Jim Bennett.

"I naturally gave him your best wishes, Mr Mayor," he continued, "and he reciprocated; and it was during this conversation that he put forward the idea of our two towns investigating the possibilities of an official twinning. Guipapont is already twinned with a West German town and another in Holland, but the Mayor, and his council as well, apparently, are keen to establish links with an English town. So it was most fortuitous I called on Monsieur Darleau that afternoon. When he discovered from me that ours was a town of similar size to theirs and that we weren't twinned with anybody, he became most enthusiastic for us to consider formal links with them. I told him I thought it an excellent idea, and would bring it before this council when next we met. That, Mr Mayor, is what I have done. I do hope we will grasp this hand of friendship extended towards us over the English Channel, and establish official twinning links with Guipapont."

"Mr Mayor, the only thing I know about this twinning business is that it's the same as any other situation where entertaining guests is concerned - it's going to cost money," said Sam Simmonds, "ratepayers money. And they won't be very keen to see their hard earned cash frittered away on nonsense such as that."

"I quite agree with Councillor Simmonds, Mr Mayor," said Dick Conway. "This council already has enough trouble in finding sufficient money to fulfill our commitments; there's no way we could justify squandering any on a tom fool idea like twinning with a French town. Anyway, if the truth be told, I don't hold with twinning; it's a load of mischievous nonsense. My father always said that there were only two races in the world - Englishmen and foreigners; and he was right. This country, Mr Mayor, has had nothing but trouble with foreign countries right through its history - especially European ones. In this century alone millions of Englishmen have died fighting them. To establish these twinning links is to spit on the graves of the brave men who fought and died for this country."

"But we've not fought the French, for heaven's sake!" cried an exasperated Ken Wilson. "Mr Mayor, they were would allies in the two World Wars - not our enemies."

"And a fat lot of good they were as well," snapped Roland Smith. "More trouble than they were worth, Mr Mayor. In the First World War they only stayed at the front 'cause our lads were behind them with bayonets, whilst in the Second they caved in almost before a shot had been fired in anger and left us to fight the Gerries on our own. No, I've got no time for the Frogs."

"Mr Mayor, I really must protest at this - this - this narrow minded bigotry."

"Who's Mr Wilson calling a bigot?" roared Smith, his face almost purple with anger. "I'll not stand for that, Mr Mayor. I'm a fair minded man - always have been. But I'm a patriot first and foremost - and like Mr Conway, I do not like foreigners."

"So you're what I just said - a bigot," snapped Wilson. Smith seemed to be about to burst a blood vessel, but whilst he was in the process of trying to turn his wrath into words, Mrs Vera Hooper got to her feet. "I still don't believe that twinning is a council matter, Mr Mayor," she opined, "but if we're making it so then perhaps I might be permitted to venture an opinion. Basically I feel that twinning is a good idea. After all, it surely has to be to the benefit of us all to broaden our outlook and our knowledge by coming into contact with the culture and the way of life of other nations. I have, though, Mr Mayor, a major criticism of the twinning pursued by most towns in this country: it nearly always lacks originality, adventure and - and I do feel this is so very important - a sense of social awareness and responsibility. What I'm getting at, Mr Mayor, is that comfortable, reasonably well off towns and villages in this country twin with similar places in France or

Germany - sometimes, perhaps, in the likes of Holland or Belgium. That's all very well as far as it goes, Mr Mayor, but I would like to feel that this council, if we decided to seek twinning links, should look beyond France, and, in fact, all of Europe. We should be bold, Mr Mayor, and make our twinning a highly significant gesture in a world where the gaps between the rich and poor nations gets ever wider. What I'm saying, Mr Mayor, is that we should forget this Guipa place and seek twinning links with a town in Ethiopia, or the Sudan or Bangladesh, or some such Third World Country as that. I'm sure that if we were to pursue such a bold policy, others would soon follow."

You've got to be joking," rasped Dick Conway, not sure whether to laugh or cry. "Mr Mayor, who in their right mind would want to pay a small fortune to go to Ethiopia? Let's face it, the whole purpose of twinning is to have a mutual booze up. I reckon in Ethiopia and the Sudan and such like, about the only drink you'll get is water - and that'll probably kill you."

"Mr Conway has totally missed the point I'm making, Mr Mayor," protested Mrs Hooper. "And probably deliberately as well," she added darkly. "What I'm trying to get over to the council is that we should not be lemming-like regarding this twinning business. Just because virtually every other place twins with a European counterpart, it doesn't mean we should do the same. If we were to twin with a town in, say, Ethiopia, we could send them - in fact, possibly, we could take them - things which would help them in their very hard lives. Food, blankets, medical supplies - all of these things and more we could take to these unfortunate people and receive, in return, those things which mark their own unique culture....."

"Like a bucket of sand and a few thousand flies," snorted Dick Conway. "Mr Mayor, I've never heard such a load of tripe in all my days. All twinnings are a waste of time in my estimation, but to even consider such links with the countries Mrs Hooper is talking about is plain daft."

"I wouldn't agree with that at all, Mr Mayor," said Ken Wilson, somewhat piously. "Mrs Hooper's idea has much merit. In fact her vision of twinning is the correct one really - the exchange of cultures, mutual help and so on. However, having said that, I do believe that links with under developed Third World Countries would be a somewhat ambitious prospect for us at present. Far better, Mr Mayor, for us to forge formal links with Guipapont in France and once we've established strong ties with them, then we could well look much farther afield for our second twinning."

"Mr Mayor, the only thing I want to forge any links with is my bed," said Sam Simmonds, wearily. "This debate has gone on long enough. All we're doing is to go round in circles. Let's make some decision on this, for heaven's sake."

"I quite agree with Mr Simmonds, Mr Mayor," retorted Wilson in his suave way. "We should make a decision on this matter - here and now. With that in mind, I propose that this council establish formal links with the French town of Guipapont." He made to sit down, but promptly straightened up again. "I would deem it a privilege, Mr Mayor, to be the - what shall I call it - well, the link man in this business. I get on very well with the Mayor of Guipapont, Mr Mayor, so feel that I would possibly be the ideal man to actually negotiate the twinning."

"Biggative bugger," muttered Roland Smith.

"Mr Wilson has proposed that we establish formal twinning links with Guipapont," droned Basil Parfitt. "Do I have a seconder?"

"Point of order, Mr Mayor," rasped Dick Conway. "We can't vote on an important resolution like this without having a full debate on it - and learning more about it, and its implications."

"Mr Mayor, what Councillor Conway says is nonsense," stormed Ken Wilson. "After all, what have we just been doing if not debating this issue? It's possible to debate for ever, Mr Mayor - and do nothing. I feel that we've given this business a very good airing, so let's now vote on it and then get on with organising this twinning."

"Assuming the council's in favour, Mr Wilson," interjected the Mayor somewhat reproachfully.

"And I don't know that the council will be in favour, Mr Mayor," snapped Dick Conway. "I shall certainly vote against it at present. The fact is, we know nothing about the implications of twinning. We don't know if it will be supported by the town. We don't know if other organisations will be interested in getting involved - which has to be important. Most of all, though, Mr Mayor, we do not know just how much all this business will cost this council. I mean, it would be absurd to vote in favour of twinning, then find we don't have enough money to carry it through. A sub-committee, Mr Mayor - that's the way, at present. We should set up a sub-committee and they should go into it all thoroughly, then report back to this council at a later date."

"I quite agree, Mr Mayor," said Sam Simmonds, desperately looking for a way of bringing the proceedings to an end. "A sub-committee's the answer."

"Yes, I think perhaps that would be the best course," agreed the Mayor.

"But Mr Mayor," cried Wilson, "this will mean that we'll waste weeks -perhaps even months!"

"Possibly, Mr Wilson. But I do feel it's important we don't rush into this business - attractive though the idea might well be," added the Mayor quickly. "No, I think a sub-committee is the best plan here. Members agree that we should set up a sub-committee to go into all the implications of a formal twinning with the French town of Guipapont?"

There were mumbled "yeses," "noes" and a fair amount of coughing. Basil Parfitt looked cross. The way things were going, he'd be lucky to get home by dawn.

"Perhaps we'd better have a vote on it," he snapped. "All in favour of setting up the sub committee. One, two, three, four, five, six.......Now, those against. One, two, three, four, five, six again. Which means I've got the casting vote. I vote for the setting up of such a sub-committee. Right," he continued briskly, "who's going to be on this committee?"

"I propose the usual members, Mr Mayor; yourself, the deputy mayor, chairman of finance and chairman of properties." Dick Conway had rattled off his proposals so quickly that there was a brief pause after he sat down as members considered it. Ken Wilson was the first to spot its weakness - from his point of view.

"But, Mr Mayor, that doesn't include me," he whined. "Surely I should be on it; after all, the entire thing is my idea. And I've background knowledge which I think will be vital to the sub-committee."

"Yes, I think it's only right that Mr Wilson be on it, Mr Mayor," said Mrs Hooper. "I feel he will have quite a bit to contribute."

"Load of rubbish, that's what he'll contribute," muttered Roland Smith.

"Yes, I think perhaps Mr Wilson should be on the committee," agreed Basil Parfitt. "He is, after all, our French expert," he added, with a hint of sarcasm in his voice. "Members agree with Mr Conway's proposals, plus Mr Wilson, for the sub-committee?"

Members did, indeed, agree. All, that is, except Roland Smith, who neither agreed nor disagreed. He just sat slumped in his seat, a doom-laden expression on his face. Basil Parfitt glanced at his watch - and winced. These meetings seemed to ramble on for ever. It was time to bring it to a close. "I trust there's no other business," he said - and when Basil Parfitt put on such a demeanour few argued with him. Not that he gave them the chance anyway. "There being no other business, ladies and gentlemen, I declare the meeting closed at 10.20."

Everybody got up from their seats and prepared for home except for Roland Smith. He just sat in his chair gazing straight ahead, blankly. Dick Conway walked around, and sat down beside him. "What's the matter, Roland?" he asked cheerfully. "You look like death warmed up."

Councillor Smith shook his head sadly. "What took hold of me Dick? I must be mad. I let that big-headed fool Wilson get up my nose, and before I know it, I'm threatening to resign. And I don't want to, Dick, I don't want to. I enjoy being on the council. I know I've threatened it in the past, but there was never any real chance that I would have to. It's different now though."

"You won't have to resign," assured Conway in a soothing tone.

"But I will. After all, there's no way that this council won't eventually propose a formal twinning with this Frog town. It might take a while, but it's bound to come. I've been around long enough to know that. Far too many people in favour of it, both on and off the council."

"Oh, yes, I reckon it'll come - sometime. But it's a long time in the future, don't you worry." Conway's tone was confident rather than soothing now. "I made sure of that when I proposed that sub-committee."

"How do you mean?"

"Well, think it through, Roland. Who's on it? Basil Parfitt for a start. Now old Basil's no great bridge builder; a conservative by nature and probably politically as well. And he's not the most energetic of Mayors, either: He won't want anything to do with this twinning nonsense whilst he's in office, for certain. And the deputy mayor's very similar. In fact, I reckon Sam Simmonds will be even less keen on it than Basil. No lover of foreigners - Sam. Dorothy Parsons will be there as chairman of properties, of course, and she'll probably be in favour of it, to start with. But you know, Dorothy; easiest thing in the world to brow beat her. And then there's the chairman of finance - me. And I shall certainly oppose twinning. We're short enough of money now. Certainly there's nothing like enough to do half what we should be doing as a council. So there's no way I shall ever support twinning, Roland. A complete waste of time and money. So our friend Mr Wilson will find himself isolated on the sub-committee. Might well come one day, of course, with some changes in the council after an election or two, but that's way to the future.''

"But it'll still mean I'll have to resign one day," muttered Smith, gloomily.

"Rubbish. After a year or two everybody'll forget you ever threatened to resign. People don't remember things for very long - you know that."

Roland Smith nodded his head. "Something in what you say, boy, I must admit. They do forget things."

"Of course they do. I reckon there's not a chance you'll have to resign from this council over twinning, Roland."

Smith got jauntily to his feet, grinning broadly. "I must say you've made me feel a fair bit better, Dick. Tell you what - you've got to pass my place on the way home; how about coming in for a quick drink?"

"Yes - all right Roland. Excellent idea. Thanks very much."

They walked briskly towards the door, Smith still looking mightily pleased with life. He glanced at his companion as they walked through the door and into the lobby which led to the street. "Over that drink we could perhaps talk about who's going to be deputy mayor to Sam Simmonds when he takes over. Only a few months away, you know. Soon be with us. How would you fancy it, Dick? You'd be the ideal man in my opinion."

"Well - I'd not really thought about it. But I could be interested," said Dick Conway as they walked out into the street, a hint of a smile playing around his lips.

# THE TREE

If there were two things in this world which councillor Albert Bingley detested, they were rain and site meetings. And the trouble was, they usually came together.

He glanced up at the sky as he clambered stiffly from his car; it was going to happen again today. The sky was black as an undertaker's hat, and the wind was freshening from the West. Still, it wasn't raining yet so with a bit of luck - and unusual brevity from the committee - they might be able to finish before it did.

He walked towards the wide, ornate, black painted gate, checked the name, "Fresh Winds", emblazoned in white upon it, considered it most apt as the rising Westerly tousled his whitening hair, opened the gate and went inside. A group of councillors and officials stood to the left of the house in a large garden which consisted of a wide expanse of grass, with a few shrubs dotted about and a large copper beech tree almost in the middle. One of their number, David Nisbet, the chief planning officer, left the group having seen his chairman come into the garden.

"Morning, Mr Bingley," he said brightly. "Rain's holding off - but not for long I'm afraid."

"No, not for long, David. That's why I think we should get this meeting over and done with as soon as possible," replied Councillor Bingley, chairman of the planning committee.

"It shouldn't take long. There aren't many members present actually."

"There never are when the weather doesn't look too good." They joined the group, standing on the lawn, amidst a flurry of 'mornings' and 'going to be a dirty day' and so on. Albert

Bingley positioned himself in the middle of them, pulled a bundle of papers from his abused pocket, and eyed the group which surrounded him.

"Well, ladies and gentlemen, I think perhaps we'd best make a start. You can just about touch the rain with a stick, so the quicker we get on with this meeting - and get it over - the better. Mr Nisbet, please."

"Thank you, Mr Chairman. As members will be aware, this site meeting has been called in order to be able to forward a recommendation to the next full meeting of the planning committee as to whether the planning application in question should be allowed or refused."

"Perhaps you would remind members of the nature of the application, and of the objections, and so forth," said the chairman, keen for the able, amiable, but often long winded Nisbet, to get to the point.

"Yes, of course, Mr Chairman," replied Nisbet, in his unruffled way. "As members will be aware, the application has been put in by Mr & Mrs Carter, who, of course, own this house to our left here, the garden of which we are now standing in. They have submitted plans for a four-bedroomed house to be built here in this garden. Now whilst we as a planning authority have no objection to the plans as such - size, lay out, materials and so on - there are considerable numbers of objections from other bodies and individuals."

"Country highways for one, no doubt," snapped Councillor Ivor Ogden.

"Well, yes, that's correct, Mr Chairman," agreed Nisbet. "They object on the grounds that it is inadvisable to have any more outlets onto this road at present." He indicated the busy Victoria Road, which lay on the other side of the garden hedge, with a rather theatrical wave of his hand.

"They always object on those grounds, Mr Chairman," said Ogden, his voice dripping with cynicism.

"That is so, Mr Chairman," agreed the planning officer. "And I fancy they'll continue to do so until a by-pass is built which will take away much of the traffic which at present uses Victoria Road, and, indeed, clutters up the town."

"By-pass? We'll all be dead by the time that's built," snorted Councillor Mrs Ethel Nugent.

"Oh, I do think Mrs Nugent's being just a little pessimistic, Mr Chairman," said Nisbet, stoically. "After all, we are down on the forward planning list for a by-pass in the foreseeable future."

Helen Nugent snorted, "Foreseeable future, Mr Chairman? Foreseeable for our great grandchildren perhaps - we'll never see it, that's for sure."

"Sadly, I do tend to agree with you," said Albert Bingley.

"Point of order, Mr Chairman," said Councillor Jim Jennings, in his husky, rather croaking voice.

At eighty, the old fellow was 'father' of the council in both years of service and age.

"Yes, Mr Jennings," replied the Chairman, in a highly respectful tone of voice. A great respecter of age and experience, was Albert Bingley.

"It's just that my old legs are playing me up a bit, Mr Chairman - they don't like all the wet weather, you know. I wonder if it would be all right if I sat down on this low wall here to my left." He indicated an ornamental wall, some two feet high and about eighteen inches wide, which ran for about ten yards across part of the garden, but appeared to serve no useful purpose at all.

"Yes, of course, Mr Jennings," agreed the chairman instantly. As the old fellow slumped down onto the wall, the chairman glanced at the chief planning officer.

"If you'd continue, Mr Nisbet."

"Thank you, Mr Chairman. To continue with the letters of opposition to this application. There is one from the next door neighbours, on both sides, claiming that the proposed house would overlook them and take their light."

"That's plain daft, Mr Chairman," stormed Councillor Joe Davidson. "It can't overlook both of them. If the house was to be built roughly where we're standing now - which is what the plan suggests - then it can only overlook the house over the fence facing us, which is thirty feet away. The other neighbour though, is on the other side of the applicants' house. There's no way they'll ever even see this building - if ever it's put up - from over there. Overlook them? Take their light? Rubbish - mischievous rubbish as well. A clear case, Mr Chairman, of somebody in a nice comfortable position in life trying to stop somebody else building a decent home for folk to live in. Makes me sick."

"I agree with Mr Davidson, Mr Chairman," croaked Jim Jennings from his low, stone perch. "There are too many people in this town trying to stop others building decent homes. And that's something we've all got a right to, you know - a decent home. That was one of the things we fought the last war for as well - 'homes fit for heroes.' Well, perhaps we didn't actually fight for that," he said, an expression of doubt flitting momentarily across his face, "but it was promised nonetheless. Yet here we are with scores of homeless people about and the council has waiting lists getting longer every day. It's a poor show, Mr Chairman, and no mistake. The only way we're ever going to sort it out is to build more homes - and I can see no reason why they shouldn't go ahead and build here. After all, it'll get somebody's name off the waiting list......"

"Mr Chairman, with respect," interjected David Nisbet, "I feel that Councillor Jennings is being perhaps a little premature in saying that the building of this house should go ahead. After all, councillors have not yet heard all the objections to the passing of this planning application - and there are many. Also, I do feel I ought to point out, Mr Chairman, that the house here will cost, I would estimate, somewhere in the region of £180,000, so it won't be occupied by somebody whose name is on the council house waiting list."

"That's beside the point, Mr Chairman," argued Jennings, doggedly. "if a house is built, then it's going to be lived in by somebody. That person will probably move from a house he's already living in which will leave that one empty for somebody else to move into - and so it goes on, right down through the line, with, at the bottom, somebody moving out of a council house and somebody else coming off the list and going into that empty house."

There was a brief silence as the small assembly tried to come to terms with the old fellow's devastating logic.

"Well - yes. There could be something in what you say, Mr Jennings," opined the chairman, at last.

"However, as Mr Nisbet pointed out, there are several other objections to the plans, objecting, I believe, on a number of other aspects of the situation, so we really should hear them before we try to come to any conclusions on the matter." The elderly councillor shrugged his shoulders in acquiescence, and tried to make himself more comfortable on his hard seat. Albert Bingley, meanwhile, nodded at the chief planning officer. "Carry on Mr Nisbet."

"Thank you, Mr Chairman," he said, urbanely. "There is a letter of objection from the Water Authority saying that until the larger main planned for this road is put in, then there should be no further development."

"That's a new one, Mr Chairman," snorted Ivor Ogden. "Just like the Water Board to think of something to stop us using water."

"They're a disgrace, the Water Board," snapped Mrs Nugent, quickly astride one of her favourite hobby horses. "The only time they ever seem able to supply water is when it's raining. A few dry days and there's a hosepipe ban - a couple of dry weeks and they turn it off altogether. I think, Mr Chairman, we should write to the Water Board in no uncertain terms and complain about the way they treat us in this town - and about their general incompetence. Furthermore, I feel we should demand....."

"Yes, yes, yes, Mrs Nugent," interjected the chairman hastily - aware that if urgent action were not taken, then the able, but voluble lady would flood them with a deluge of words - "everything you say is, of course, quite correct. But this is really the province of the general purposes committee - not plans. Our brief, at the moment, is simply to note the objection from the Water Board regarding the plan under discussion today."

"Yes, but....."

"Thank you, Mrs Nugent," interjected Albert Bingley once again - forcibly this time. "Carry on Mr Nisbet," he said, in a tone of voice which silenced even the valiant Ethel Nugent - though she did continue to mutter in the background.

"Thank you, Mr Chairman," said Nisbet, somewhat wearily now. "We also have letters of complaint from the Civic Society, the 'Men of the Trees,' the Council for the Preservation of Rural England, Friends of the Earth and the Wildfowl Trust, all objecting to the application on the grounds that to grant it would mean the chopping down of the copper beech just behind us."

He turned and indicated a fine, sturdy tree close to the middle of the lawn, its copper coloured leaves twisting frantically in the rising wind.

"Did I hear you say the Wildfowl Trust?" enquired Ivor Ogden a look of surprise on his face. "I mean to say - what has a copper beech tree, at least twenty miles from the coast, got to do with the Wildfowl Trust?"

"I suppose ducks perch in the tree on their way South - or North perhaps; or whichever way they happen go be going at the time," said Jim Jennings.

"Rubbish, ducks don't perch in trees," rasped Councillor Miss Helen Hinton. "Water is what they like - obviously."

David Nisbet looked puzzled regarding the conversation for a few seconds, but then his face brightened as he understood what had happened. "I'm sorry, Mr Chairman, but members seem to have misunderstood what I said. I did not refer to the Wildfowl Trust, but to the Willfell Trust, which is, I believe, a recently formed organisation in the town - funded by the estate of the late Mr Henry Willfell of Langley Manor - dedicated to the preservation of all aspects of the countryside locally, which includes trees, naturally."

"Thank you for that clarification, Mr Nisbet," said the chairman, gazing at the threatening looking sky. "Now, if we can get on, the rain's going to be upon us fairly soon, I would say."

"Well, as I was saying, Mr Chairman," continued Nisbet, "We've had all these objections from these various organisations concerning the inevitable chopping down of the copper beech should we grant planning permission. It is, as you can see, a very fine specimen and is, in the opinion of the planning department, the one real element regarding the application which might cause the committee to refuse the application. The other objections - highway problems, water and overlooking neighbours and so on - are not really sufficient, in our estimation, for us to recommend the application be refused. But that tree is a different matter. The outcry there would be should it be cut down leads us, in the planning department, towards the opinion that possibly the application should be refused."

"Trees, trees, trees - that's all we ever hear about in this town," rasped Joe Davidson. "I reckon if half the people around here had to choose between chopping down a man or a tree, they'd cut down the man."

"Trees are important, Mr Chairman," chipped in Helen Hinton. "They're our heritage. They were planted by our forebears to improve the world in which we live, so it's our duty to protect them. Certainly this lovely copper beech must be protected."

"That's all very well, Mr Chairman," argued Davidson, "but we've got to let just a little bit of reality come into our judgement. Let's face it, if our forebears, as Miss Hinton calls them, had refused to chop down every tree that got in their way, then this town now wouldn't even be the size of a hamlet. There wouldn't be half a dozen houses here. This copper beech is a nice enough tree, but there's scores more like it about. In fact, there's a couple down there at the bottom of the garden." He indicated two rather insignificant trees close to the far hedge of the large garden, both puny in comparison to the fine specimen which was the subject of discussion.

"Is there a tree preservation order on it, Mr Chairman?"

wheezed Jim Jennings from his stone seat. Albert Bingley looked at a plumpish young woman standing beside the chief planning officer. "Your department, Miss Clarke, I think."

"Thank you, Mr Chairman," replied Myra Clarke, who spent most of her working life gazing at trees on behalf of the council. "In actual fact, surprising at it might seem when one looks at such a splendid copper beech, there isn't a TPO on it. That's obviously something which should be rectified - in my opinion."

"If there's no preservation order on it, Mr Chairman, then chop the blasted tree down," said Jim Jennings. "Then there can be a decent house built here in a proper manner. I propose we recommend to the full committee that these plans be passed."

"I second that, Mr Chairman," snapped Joe Davidson.

"I don't know, Mr Chairman; I fancy we'll be in trouble if we chop this tree down." Ivor Ogden shook his head as he said the words. "You know what people around here are like when it comes to trees, Mr Chairman. I mean - we've got more than our share of nutters when it comes to trees. Having said that, I'm sympathetic to Mr Jennings feelings that the house should be built. Perhaps we could compromise in some way. Perhaps we could - perhaps we could ......" His face suddenly lit up; "perhaps we could dig it up and plant it somewhere else, Mr Chairman!" he cried triumphantly.

Albert Bingley looked perplexed. He was no expert on trees - one of the few who would, in fact, admit to such a deficiency in a town which appeared to abound with 'tree experts' - but he had a feeling that Ivor Ogden's suggestion was plain daft. He glanced across at Myra Clarke. "I wouldn't have thought such an operation possible, Miss Clarke," he said tentatively. "Would I be correct?"

"Perfectly correct, Mr Chairman," she stated authoritively. "It would be impossible to transplant a tree of that size and age. Even if we could lift it with all its roots intact - which is highly unlikely as they will have spread a great distance on all sides of it - the tree would almost certainly die if put elsewhere."

"With such confirmation from our expert, Mr Ogden, I fear your idea is a non-starter," said the Chairman gravely.

"With that in mind, Mr Chairman, I propose the plan be rejected," said Helen Hinton, "I feel......."

"Just a minute, Miss Hinton," interjected Albert Bingley, "we've already got a proposition from Mr Jennings, seconded by Mr Davidson, that we pass the plan."

"That means the tree would have to be chopped down, Mr Chairman, which is intolerable," persisted the rather strident Councillor Hinton.

"Obviously the tree would have to be chopped down if the plans are passed," retorted the chairman rather testily, "but you're jumping the gun - we haven't had a vote yet."

"Move the vote be taken, Mr Chairman," intoned Jim Jennings.

"Yes, good idea," agreed Bingley. "The proposition is, ladies and gentlemen, that the plan be passed. All those in favour please show."

Councillors Jennings and Davidson raised their hands in unison. "Two," droned the Chairman. "Against?"

Councillors Mrs Nugent and Miss Hinton quickly thrust their arms into the air, whilst Ivor Ogden sheepishly and falteringly did likewise.

"Three," said the Chairman. "The motion is defeated."

"Which means the plans are rejected," said Helen Hinton brightly.

"Not necessarily," retorted Ivor Ogden. "All that vote means is that the plans can't be passed if it means chopping down the copper beech. If there's any way the house can be built with the tree remaining where it is, then the plans could still be passed - that's correct Mr Chairman, isn't it?"

"Well, yes, - yes, I suppose it is, Mr Ogden." The chairman glanced at David Nisbet for confirmation.

"As I see it, Mr Chairman, Mr Ogden is correct," replied Nisbet. "We would appear to have established that the tree must not be cut down - that's the first thing. Oh, and on that point, is it the wish of the sub-committee that a recommendation go forward to the full committee that a tree preservation order be put on this copper beech?"

"Members agree?" asked the Chairman.

Councillors Nugent and Hinton did, Councillors Jennings and Davidson did not, and Councillor Ogden didn't really know whether he agreed or not. Albert Bingley glanced at the angry looking sky; he was sure he felt rain on his face. It was time to hurry this meeting along.

"Carried," he snapped. "Recommendation to go forward to the full committee that a TPO be put on this tree. Carry on Mr Nisbet."

"Thank you, Mr Chairman. As I said just now, we have established that the tree must not be touched. We have not, though, necessarily decided that the plans be rejected. However, having said that, I don't really see how the proposed house can be built if the copper beech is to remain where it is."

"If we've got to keep the blasted tree," grunted Jim Jennings, "why don't we allow them to build the house in front of the tree? That seems to be a reasonable compromise to me, Mr Chairman."

Nisbet looked aghast. "That's impossible, Mr Chairman - absolutely impossible," he rasped. "That would bring the house almost up to the road, and well in front of the building line. We can't allow that, Mr Chairman - it would open the floodgates the length of Victoria Road. There'd be planning applications coming in left, right and centre to extend homes in all directions, to put bungalows on the front lawns and all sorts. No, Mr Chairman, we cannot allow any building forward of the existing line on this road."

"Well, how about building it behind the damned tree then?" persisted Jennings. "Can't see anything wrong with that, Mr Chairman."

"Not on, Mr Chairman, I'm afraid," retorted the chief planning officer quickly. "To start with it would be most unwise of this committee to allow building well to the rear of the great majority of houses on this road. Once again it would set an unfortunate - perhaps even a dangerous - precedent. Quite apart from that, though, the main sewer goes underneath the back garden here, as it does for most of the length of the road; so obviously we can't have a house built over the main sewer, Mr Chairman."

"No - quite so," agreed Albert Bingley, wearily, wishing there was a way in which he could bring the meeting to a conclusion. It looked as if it could hammer down at any moment. "In actual fact, Mr Chairman, if I may be permitted to say so, I really don't think there's any way in which this plan can be permitted to go ahead. It seems to be this sub-committee's view - quite rightly in my opinion - that the copper beech must be preserved. So if that is the case, the house obviously cannot be built, as the only spot where it can be put is where the tree stands."

"Quite so, Mr Nisbet," said the chairman quickly, seeing a way of bringing this tiresome meeting to a close before they all got soaked. "As the chief planning officer says, ladies and gentlemen, there's no possible way this plan can be allowed to go forward, so can I have a formal proposition it be rejected?" He looked expectantly at his committee. Helen Hinton began to raise her arm, but before she could say anything, Ivor Ogden proposed an idea. "I agree that the tree should stay, Mr Chairman, as you know, but surely there's a way a compromise can be reached. Surely the plan can be revised for the house to be built - well, sort of - well sort of around the tree." The final words were said without conviction.

"Yes, that's a good idea," agreed Jim Jennings enthusiastically. "As I've said, Mr Chairman, I believe this house should be built. A structure of the size envisaged will be an asset to this road - and to the town. This committee though, have already decided we've got to keep the copper beech; so the only solution is to plan the house in such a way that it sort of curves around the house - sort of banana-shape."

"You can't have a banana-shaped house, Mr Chairman" rasped Joe Davidson. "That'll look absolutely daft."

"Well, I don't know that it should be built banana-shaped, Mr Chairman," said Ivor Ogden brightly, pleased that somebody else felt the co-existence of both the tree and the new house was possible. "But I do feel that Mr Jennings' idea does have merit. For instance, there must be some way that this house can be designed so that the bulk of it lies each side of the tree, whilst these two halves - for want of a better description - could be joined together by a narrow portion which lies behind the copper beech; if you see what I mean, Mr Chairman."

"I'm not sure I do Mr Ogden," retorted the chairman, testily.

"This sounds like a most peculiar house to me." A raindrop splattered onto the middle of his agenda. He glanced quickly at the sky; there were a lot more to come, and very soon. He returned his gaze to the gathering of councillors and officials. "Still, if the committee wants to pursue the possibility of getting the applicants to submit fresh plans which will accommodate both the tree and a re-shaped house, then so be it. All I ask is that such a resolution is proposed right away - before we get wet through." The committee knew Albert Bingley very well; he'd been on the council for almost twenty years and chairman of planning for the past six. He was an amiable, courteous man, and generally very patient. But when he spoke in that certain, clipped fashion, they knew he was in no mood to be argued with; he wanted a proposition, and that was what he would get.

"I propose that the planning department liaise with the applicant and get him to submit plans which will ensure that the copper beech remains," said Jim Jennings authoritively.

"Seconded, Mr Chairman," snapped Helen Hinton. "Not that I'm convinced that this is a good idea - or even a feasible one. I frankly don't believe it's possible to come up with a design which doesn't look ludicrous, whilst retaining the tree. Still, that's a problem for the applicants and the planning department, not for us. The only important thing, to my mind, is that the copper beech remains in all its splendour."

"There are one or two problems here as I see it Mr Chairman," opined Ivor Ogden. "To start with....."

"Thank you, Mr Ogden," interjected Albert Bingley, "but I feel we've had ample discussion on this matter, and I'm not prepared to allow any more. We have a proposition and I shall now put it to the vote. Those in favour, please show."

Jim Jennings' right arm shot up into the air, Helen Hinton's was raised sluggishly, whilst Ethel Nugent raised hers rather sheepishly, not terribly keen to be seen supporting such a silly idea, but aware that if they didn't reach some conclusion then they'd all end up wet through. As her hand reached its zenith, she assuaged her conscience by convincing herself that the bizarre plan would never go through the full planning committee.

"Three", said the Chairman. "And against?"

He looked at Joe Davidson and Ivor Ogden. The former, though, stood gazing morosely into the distance; he thought the entire business so daft, he refused to vote at all. In fact, he began to wonder whether it wasn't time for him to come off a committee that could vote for a tree instead of a decent house, and then decide to build some absurd contraption around it. The latter gazed back at the chairman for a few seconds, then looked away. He was so confused with the entire business that he didn't know whether he was for it or against.

"None. The proposal is carried."

"I accept the decision of the committee, naturally, Mr Chairman," said David Nisbet, considerable disquiet evident in his normally soft, level voice. "However, I must say that this is all very irregular. I really don't see how it's possible to retain the copper beech and build the house, Mr Chairman. To construct such a building would mean the breaking of half a dozen basic planning laws - perhaps more. The entire idea's a non-starter, Mr Chairman - I have to say that."

"Well, that's for you to decide in liaison, with the applicants," snapped the Chairman. "We have merely passed a resolution that an attempt should be made to accommodate both the tree and the new house on this site - with the tree taking priority, of course."

The chief planning officer shrugged his shoulders. "Very well,

Mr Chairman," he acquiesced.

"Good - that's settled then," said Albert Bingley, almost jovially. They had finished the meeting without getting soaked - though the rain was now falling quite heavily.

"I declare the meeting closed, and thank you for your attendance, ladies and gentlemen."

The words had scarce passed his lips before the assembled throng galloped for the road, and their parked cars, even the ancient Jim Jennings showing a fair turn of speed despite his ailing legs.

As Albert Bingley reached his car - which was parked farthest away because he was last to arrive - the rain began to fall heavily, carried on a South West wind little short of gale force. He clambered quickly inside, put the key into the ignition, and started up.

He glanced to his left, at the garden where they had just spent the last half hour, then to the open road on his right, pulled the car onto it, and shook his head sadly. He had known greater wastes of time, but he couldn't really remember when. Their proposal of the morning would be put to the full planning committee and would be rejected as a whole; the copper beech would be retained, a preservation order would be put on it, but plans for the house - no matter in what shape it was presented - would not be passed. The applicants would then appeal to the Ministry, where their appeal would probably be upheld, the tree condemned to the chain-saw, and within twelve months a fine, new house of traditional style would stand where they had stood that morning.

"Oh, well," he muttered to himself as he steered his car towards home, "that's grass-root democracy at work, I suppose."

-----------

# THE CURTAINS

Sandra Miles was pleased. When first looking at the agenda for the monthly meeting of the properties committee, she had anticipated a long session - perhaps right through to eleven o'clock or even beyond. But the reality had been so very different. Of course, 'apologies for absence' held the key to the unexpected brevity of the meeting. For the one apology for non-attendance had come from Edward Hancock, a man who had a rare talent for making the obvious, obscure, and the simple, complicated, and who could add an hour to any meeting. However, his had not been a full apology; rather he had said he would definitely be late because he had to attend the Annual General Meeting of the bowling club, but hoped to get to the properties committee meeting before it finished.

Sandra Miles was convinced that it was this threat of his probable arrival at some time or other which had led to an unusually brisk and well-disciplined contribution from the other members of the committee, all of them desiring to finish the meeting before he arrived. She glanced at her watch; only five minutes past nine and they'd almost achieved it.

"We come to the last item on the agenda, any other business," she said quickly, "I believe there is one item, Mr Hughes."

"Thank you, Mr Chairman," replied Paul Hughes, the town clerk. A young, earnest man, he took both his job and himself extremely seriously indeed. "I've received a letter from the town's Gilbert and Sullivan Society concerning problems they had with the stage curtains in the town hall during their show which finished last week."

"What show was that?" asked Councillor Aubrey Spry,

slouched in his seat towards the back of the council chamber.

The town clerk looked a trifle nonplussed. "Well - I don't really know, Mr Chairman. I'm not into Gilbert and Sullivan to be quite honest. Having said that, I must admit that I should know, seeing as I received the customary invitation to the Mayor and council to attend on Civic night. Unfortunately I was unable to go, and the Mayor's not here this evening. I don't know if any other councillor went to the show?"

"I went, Mr Chairman", replied the veteran Councillor Ronald Lashbrook, wheezing away enthusiastically. "It was very good as well. Thoroughly enjoyed it, the missus and me."

"That's splendid, Mr Lashbrook," said the Chairman in a respectful tone. "Perhaps you would tell us which Gilbert and Sullivan operetta they put on this year."

"The Importance of Being Earnest, Mr Chairman," replied the old councillor instantly. "One of my favourites that - and the missus's as well."

"That's not Gilbert and Sullivan," rasped Aubrey Spry. "That's Oscar Wilde - and that's a play not an opera."

"I think perhaps Councillor Lashbrook is thinking of the dramatic society's recent production, Mr Chairman," explained the town clerk, trying to be helpful. "I remember he, and Mrs Lashbrook, attended that, along with the Mayor, myself, and a few other councillors. About two months ago, I fancy."

"Yes, that's what he's thinking of," agreed councillor Cyril Coleman, a long, beanpole of a man, who seemed to entwine himself around his chair rather than sit in it. "A load of rubbish it was, as well. Never been so bored in my life; the acting was shocking, hardly anybody on the stage could remember their lines, and it was freezing cold."

"It's always cold in the town hall," snapped Aubrey Spry.

"I've been freezing in there in June. It beats me how anybody ever hires the damned place. It's time the heating was sorted out."

"Actually the heating problems of the town hall are on the agenda for the next meeting of the Forward Planning Committee, Mr Chairman," said the town clerk quickly. "Hopefully we'll then be able to formulate some future policy to solve the problem once and for all."

"When's that?" asked Spry.

"When's what?" retorted the town clerk.

"The next meeting of the forward planning committee, for heaven's sake," rasped an exasperated Councillor Spry; he was never a man to whom patience came easily.

"Well, we haven't fixed a date yet, Mr Chairman," replied Paul Hughes, somewhat uncomfortably. "We just seem to have had so much to do recently."

"He'll have me in tears in a minute," muttered Cyril Coleman to his near neighbour, Ronald Lashbrook. The veteran councillor didn't hear, though, his entire concentration centred on trying to remember what Gilbert and Sullivan production he had seen the previous week.

"It seems to me, Mr Chairman, that this forward planning committee is a farce," ranted Spry. "I mean it's been formed for several years - five at least - yet how often has it met? I can't remember the last time there was a meeting. Certainly there's not been one since I've been on it - and that's a couple of years. So, when was the last time it met?"

The chairman looked searchingly at the clerk. "Well, Mr Hughes?"

Paul Hughes cleared his throat nervously. "Well, Mr Chairman," he said slowly, his voice very soft, "I do believe that, in actual fact, despite many wide ranging ideas for the future having come from the council, and indeed, having been put to the council from several outside bodies, ideas of considerable relevance to the town and the chargepayers......."

"For heaven's sake, get to the point," roared an angry Aubrey Spry, "we've not got all night."

"I was about to, Mr Chairman," retorted the town clerk, rare annoyance in his voice. "The fact, as far as I'm aware, is that the forward planning committee has never met."

"Never?" spluttered Spry.

"As far as I'm aware, Mr Chairman," retorted the town clerk, his voice returning to its normal urbanity.

"Then why, Mr Chairman," continued Spry, in his terrier-like way, "do we go through the time wasting farce every May at the Annual Meeting of appointing members to a committee that never meets? Why does the town clerk speak of putting things on an agenda which will never be discussed? I've been on this council fifteen years and seen some pretty stupid things, but I've never come across anything as daft as this."

"Well, obviously, Mr Chairman, if we appoint a committee then it can meet should the council wish it to and if we draw up an agenda then we're prepared should the council decide to call a meeting of the committee," defended Paul Hughes. "The fact that it hasn't met as yet over - over the years - is, with respect, irrelevant. It's like having a fire extinguisher isn't it, Mr Chairman? I mean, we've got fire extinguishers in this chamber, and in this building, but we never use them - and hopefully we'll never have to. But......"

"We did once," interjected Cyril Coleman. "Remember it well."

"Remember what, Mr Coleman?" asked the chairman sharply;

she was getting somewhat frustrated at the way the meeting was degenerating into a rambling squabble.

"When we used a fire extinguisher, Mr Chairman," retorted Coleman in exasperated fashion, as if amazed that his meaning had not been understood.

"I don't ever recall this," said the town clerk.

"Oh, it was before your time," said Coleman. "Years ago it was. A car caught fire outside in the street whilst we were in the middle of a meeting of a sub-committee. The chairman then - poor old Harry Dawkins, dead and gone now - grabbed an extinguisher and rushed out into the road." He stopped suddenly, and shook his head, a wry smile playing around his lips.

"What happened then?" asked Councillor Mrs Clare Newman, who had just dragged her attention away from the agenda of the following evening's planning committee, which lay before her.

"The car burnt out, that's what happened," snorted Cyril Coleman. "The extinguisher didn't work."

"That's extraordinary, Mr Chairman," said a bemused Paul Hughes. "Those extinguishers are checked every year. In fact, I....."

"Mr Chairman, what are we doing talking about fire extinguishers?" snapped Aubrey Spry. "I thought we were discussing the fact that the forward planning committee has never met."

"Well, yes, that's correct, Mr Chairman," replied the town clerk somewhat wearily. "However, I brought the purchasing of fire extinguishers into the debate to provide an analogy as to the wisdom of looking to the future."

"Then it's a poor analogy, Mr Chairman," retorted Spry, "What after all, is the similarity between the purchasing of fire extinguishers and the fact that the forward planning committee has never met? And - and another thing," continued the councillor quite excitedly, a new train of thought having suddenly come to him, "the town clerk talks about the appointment of this committee being an act of wisdom in looking to the future, yet the committee itself, which is all about planning for the future, never meets. I've never heard anything as daft in all my life."

"The reason why this committee has never been convened, Mr Chairman," retorted the town clerk sternly, "is simply because the council has never instructed me to do so."

"But that's not the point, Mr Chairman," persisted Councillor Spry. "What I want....."

"You're quite right, Mr Spry, that is not the point," interjected the chairman, rather crossly. "In fact the point we should be discussing was lost several minutes ago. We should be discussing the letter which we have received from the Gilbert and Sullivan Society - and that is what we shall do, without going off at any more tangents. Mr Hughes, please."

"Thank you, Mr Chairman. Well, as I said just now, the letter concerns problems which the society experienced with the stage curtains during their final show last Saturday night. It says....."

"Macbeth!" cried Ronald Lashbrook.

"I beg your pardon, Mr Lashbrook?"

"Macbeth, Mr Chairman, that was the name of the Gilbert and Sullivan show we saw last week. I knew it would come to me if I pondered long enough."

Sandra Miles smiled wanly, quickly decided that to disagree with the aged councillor would prolong the meeting possibly well into the night as he returned to his pondering, so nodded gravely. "Yes - quite. Thank you, Mr Lashbrook," she replied gently, "carry on Mr Hughes, please."

"Thank you, Mr Chairman. Well, regarding these curtains; it appears that something went wrong with the smooth running of the left hand one along the - the - well, the sort of runners they run on. One of the cast grabbed hold of the curtain to pull it to the centre and so screen the stage, and the entire curtain came down on him. It caused quite a bit of alarm at the time and, according to the letter, ruined the final curtain call of the show. So the society are demanding that the entire curtains around the stage area be renewed, as they are, according to them, rotten beyond repair."

He coughed somewhat nervously. "They are also, Mr Chairman, demanding a reduction in the hire charges for the hall because of the incident."

"I was waiting for that," came a voice from the back of the chamber. Depression engulfed the gathering as the chairman and town clerk looked towards the back of the room and members of the committee turned to gaze behind them to see who had caused the interruption to their deliberations. Not that they needed to look; they knew that raucous voice all right.

"Good evening, Mr Hancock," said the chairman, rather icily.

"Good evening, Mr Chairman," replied the late arrival, politely. "I apologise for being so late, but I did tell the clerk that I would never be able to get here for the beginning of this meeting. I'm glad to see, though, that I'm not too late to make some contribution to the proceedings." All the time he had been talking, he had been moving forward towards his usual seat on the right of the chamber. He reached it, dropped his agenda and minutes on the deck in front of him, sat down, and immediately had his say.

"I repeat my comment of a couple of minutes ago, Mr Chairman," he trumpeted in his usual confident, not to say, bombastic fashion. "I was waiting for a demand from the Gilbert and Sullivan Society for a reduction in the hire charges of the town hall. I'd have almost been disappointed if they'd not made one; after all they've done so on some pretext or other for the past few years. Last year they wanted a reduction because just a tiny bit of the stage collapsed with dry rot; the year before that they were complaining, and demanding a discount, because a fuse blew in the kitchen and they couldn't make tea one evening; and I believe, the year before that they tried to get out of paying the full amount because the caretaker was in a hurry to go home at the end of one of the shows and inadvertently locked some of the performers in the hall. Now, I reckon...."

"Point of order Mr Chairman!" cried Clare Newton.

"Yes, Mrs Newton?" asked Sandra Miles, somewhat surprised. The admirable Mrs Newton, although a regular antagonist of Hancock's, was not usually very much to the fore in the 'point of order' stakes.

"Well, Mr Chairman," she continued, "is it in order for Mr Hancock to go on about this business when he was not here when the town clerk described the contents of the letter from the Gilbert and Sullivan Society? After all, he's talking about something he knows nothing about."

"Rubbish, Mr Chairman," retorted Hancock. "I heard every word the town clerk said regarding the curtains. I was standing inside the door of the chamber, taking off my coat, and listening, for at least a couple of minutes before I spoke. It seems to me that Mrs Newton is just trying to stifle free speech - and I've a good idea I know why."

"What's that meant to mean?" snapped Clare Newton, her thinnish face white with anger. One day, thought the chairman to herself, Councillor Mrs Newton would go through a meeting without getting angry with Edward Hancock.

"I fancy Mrs Newton knows what I mean, Mr Chairman," insisted Hancock. "It's simply that her husband is a stalwart member of the local Gilbert and Sullivan Society. Is that not correct, Mrs Newton?"

"Mr Hancock, I don't think that this form of debate is right or proper," reproached the chairman.

"The fact that Mr Newton is a member of the society is nothing whatever to do with this committee. Mrs Newton is perfectly within her rights to enter into debate on this matter just as she is obviously within her rights to raise her point of order as she did just now. Having said that, you also, Mr Hancock, have a right to express your views on any matter which comes up for discussion in this chamber whether or not you are in full possession of all the facts. So, with that in mind, I reject Mrs Newton's point of order."

"Thank you, Mr Chairman," replied Hancock, a rare tone of meekness in his voice.

"Surely she should declare an interest, Mr Chairman," snapped Aubrey Spry slumped down in his seat.

"I beg your pardon, Mr Spry?"

"Mrs Newton - she should declare an interest. If her husband is a member of the Gilbert and Sullivan Society - and I must admit, I hadn't realised it until Mr Hancock said - then she must declare an interest, and then withdraw from the chamber before we discuss the matter of the curtains."

Sandra Miles looked perplexed; she always hated any discussions on declaring of interest.

"I wouldn't have thought Mrs Newton needs to declare an interest on this matter, Mr Spry," replied the chairman, the tone of her voice not nearly as confident as the words she used.

"Of course, not, Mr Chairman," retorted Clare Newton. "After all, pecuniary interest is the basis of declaring an interest - and there's no way I can gain financially from this business."

"Yes there is," persisted Aubrey Spry.

"How?" Mrs Newton managed to make the single syllabled word pregnant with hostility and anger. Such things, though, were lost on Aubrey Spry.

"Because you live with your husband, so you're his partner; therefore, any financial benefits he gets naturally come to you as well - is that no so Mr Chairman?"

"This is absolute nonsense, Mr Chairman," rasped Councillor Newton. "I mean, my husband's not seeking any financial gain from this council. Merely, the Gilbert and Sullivan Society, of which he's a member, is asking for a rebate because of the problems they had with the curtains. No matter how much the council decides to refund on the hire charges, there's no way it can benefit him by even a penny. So therefore, there's no way it can benefit me. Mr Spry's objection is absolute nonsense."

"I'm not so sure, Mr Chairman," said Cyril Coleman, thoughtfully. "I'm not saying, of course, that Mrs Newton will take personal gain in any way from anything this committee might recommend; there's no possibility of that happening, I'm well aware of that. But the fact remains that although Mrs Newton's husband doesn't have a direct financial interest in the Gilbert and Sullivan Society, he is still deeply involved with them. So any gain, financial or otherwise, which comes the way of the society, must in some way benefit him - perhaps by way of a better quality costume in the next production or a more professional orchestra to sing to, and that sort of thing. As I say, no direct financial gain to Mr Newton, but benefit nonetheless and, as Mrs Newton is his wife, then anything which benefits him, must indirectly benefit her. So I feel she should declare an interest and leave the chamber before we discuss the problem of the curtains."

Sandra Miles still looked perplexed. "Well, I still don't feel that Mrs Newton needs to declare an interest - but perhaps you can give us some guidance on this, Mr Hughes."

The town clerk also looked perplexed. "It's - it's a little difficult, Mr Chairman. The law always seems to me to be somewhat vague regarding declaring an interest. It's couched in such ambiguous terms that I really wouldn't like to hazard an opinion as to whether Mrs Newton should declare an interest or not."

The Chairman now looked exasperated. A typical, ambivalent Peter Hughes reply, she mused. Suddenly, she made a decision; there was only one way to sort it out, and she would put it into operation immediately. "We will take a vote on the matter," she snapped. "Mrs Newton not to vote, of course. All those in favour of Mrs Newton declaring an interest and leaving the meeting; three. Now, all those opposed to Mrs Newton having to declare an interest." She immediately thrust her right arm into the air. "Three again," she said. "So the vote is tied. I therefore use my casting vote - a vote in favour of Mrs Newton not having to declare an interest. Now perhaps we can get on."

Aubrey Spry was not to be so easily thrust aside. "Point of order, Mr Chairman," he barked.

"What is it, Mr Spry?" retorted Sandra Miles, testily."

"Well, with respect, Mr Chairman," he said firmly. "I'm not at all sure you had the right to a casting vote in this instance."

"What do you mean, I hadn't the right? That's absolute nonsense, Mr Spry. A chairman of any committee always has the right to a casting vote should the initial vote be tied. This vote was tied, so I broke the deadlock with my casting vote - which is as it should be."

"With respect, Mr Chairman, I think you're wrong. We had such a situation as this many years ago - before you were on the council, I fancy," he added, somewhat acidly. "We established then, as I recall, that the chairman of a committee could not vote, then have the casting vote. Or, in other words, the chairman of a committee can only vote once. Only the Mayor, when chairing a full council, can use a casting vote as you did just now. But you don't have to take my word for it, Mr Chairman - it's all in standing orders."

"Then we shall consult them," rasped Sandra Miles, her face white and taut with anger. An efficient woman, she did not take kindly to anybody questioning her decision. Those who had the little booklet with them, turned to the relevant clause, whilst those who didn't waited to be informed. The chairman gazed at the wordy paragraph which covered voting, and casting votes, and so on, but found that she was so annoyed with the entire business in general and with Aubrey Spry in particular - that she was unable to concentrate on the words before her eyes. She looked quickly at the town clerk.

"This is your province, Mr Hughes. Please tell us exactly what standing orders say in terms of 'casting votes'," she snapped.

The town clerk did not look happy. Deciphering standing orders, as far as he was concerned had all the joy of having a tooth extracted without anaesthetic. Not for the first time, he was to claim ignorance because the rules of the council had been drafted long before he had appeared upon the scene as clerk and, possibly more unfortunately, because they were couched in jargon which would have tested the translation powers of a pre-war solicitor.

"There are problems in deciding exactly what the standing order on 'casting votes' actually says Mr Chairman," he said, a little hesitantly. "The way it's written, and the somewhat antiquated language used, makes it all somewhat ambiguous. Frankly, it could probably be argued that Mr Spry's interpretation is correct; on the other hand, though, it is possible that your action in voting twice is also perfectly correct. It's all so very difficult - and of course, was drafted long before I came to this authority."

"That's no end of help," muttered a frustrated Cyril Coleman to nobody in particular.

"Well, as I read this standing order, Mr Chairman, Mr Spry is right," opined Edward Hancock in his stentorian way. "You shouldn't have used your vote twice. It might not have been your intention, Mr Chairman, but in actual fact it seems to me that you have abused your position somewhat."

Sandra Miles was reasonably patient - some might even say, long suffering - but there was a limit to her forbearance. She was totally fed-up with the nit picking nonsense coming from many members, their time wasting, and their trivial approach - and showed it in a rare flash of anger.

"Mr Hancock, how dare you accuse me of abusing my position. I have been a member of this council longer than you have, and have occupied the chair of various committees on several occasions," she rasped. "I have always approached my duties with a total honesty of intention and what decisions I have been called upon to make have always been arrived at after careful and deep thought."

"I meant no offence, Mr Chairman," replied a slightly chastened Hancock, "but...."

"You might not have meant offence, Mr Hancock, but you've certainly given it," retorted the chairman. "Still, enough of all this. We have discussed this nonsense long enough. As everybody seems to be interpreting the standing order in a different way, I shall make my own interpretation - which will also be my ruling from the chair. As far as I'm concerned, standing orders state that I'm justified in using my casting vote in the way I did - so that's an end to the matter. The vote that Mrs Newton be allowed to remain and take part in any debate on the town hall curtains, is valid - and that is an end to it."

She gazed belligerently at, firstly, Edward Hancock, then Aubrey Spry. They said not a word.

"Right, Mr Hughes, let us get on, for heaven's sake," she snapped.

"Thank you, Mr Chairman," said the town clerk, urbanely. "As I was saying just now, the Gilbert and Sullivan Society want a reduction in the hire charge of the town hall because of the problems with the curtains. Also, of course, we have to decide what we're going to do about the curtains. According to the town hall supervisor, the curtains are, to use his phrase, 'rotten as a pear', and will have to be replaced. That will cost a lot of money, Mr Chairman, and ....."

"Where is the town hall supervisor this evening, Mr Chairman?" interjected Edward Hancock, apparently unabashed by his previous joust with Sandra Miles. He indicated the empty chair where Douglas Rawson, the supervisor, usually sat during meetings; "he should be here tonight to give us a report on these damned curtains."

"Unfortunately Mr Rawson's on holiday this week, Mr Chairman," explained Hughes. "However, he has left me a few notes regarding the matter."

"What's the use of notes?" snapped Hancock, scornfully. "You can't ask questions of notes. And there are questions to be asked - many of them. What's the cost of new curtains, for one? Can the old ones be repaired? What caused them to rip in the first place? These things need to be asked, Mr Chairman - and probably much more besides. And there's obviously no way these questions can be asked if Mr Rawson isn't here."

"So what are you suggesting, Mr Hancock?" asked the Chairman, again icily.

"Simply that we defer discussion of this business until our meeting next month, Mr Chairman, when hopefully, Mr Rawson will be here to tell us exactly what the problems are and what he feels should be done to put things right."

"I agree with Mr Hancock, Mr Chairman," said Aubrey Spry. "We've got to have the full facts before we can discuss this - and take decisions."

"Nonsense Mr Chairman," snapped Clare Newton. "Mr Hughes says he's got notes regarding these curtains - which is surely all we need. Once he's given us the information he's got, then we can decide what to do about it. And I do feel we should decide something this evening - and get something done. After all, Winter's almost here now and the town hall - and the stage of course - will be used quite a bit. There's the dramatic society, the Boy Scout Gang Show, the - er - the Gilbert and Sullivan Society Christmas Carol Concert and many more things. So the stage - and curtains to draw across it - is going to be essential during the next three months or so. That's why it's so important we do something about the curtains right away."

"That's all very well, Mr Chairman," retorted Edward Hancock, "but I reckon it's more important to ensure that we spend chargepayers money wisely, than it is to rush things just to help the dramatic society - and the Gilbert and Sullivan Society," he added pointedly. "Not having stage curtains might cause them a touch of inconvenience, but that's all - it's something which can easily be overcome. After all there's nothing vital in having stage curtains."

"Mr Chairman, Mr Hancock is talking absolute tripe!" cried Mrs Newton angrily. "He obviously knows not the slightest thing about stage work because if he did he'd be well aware that it's impossible to put on a play or show, or even a concert for that matter, without stage curtains. Mr Chairman, I do feel...."

"Move next business, Mr Chairman," interjected Cyril Coleman, totally fed-up with the entire business. Sandra Miles was likewise fed-up, frustrated and exasperated with it all, but she was well aware that they couldn't just move on to the next business - which was to declare the meeting closed - until some decision was taken as to what they were going to do about the stage curtains.

"Sadly, Mr Coleman, it's not quite that simple," she explained in a tone of voice which lay somewhere between impatience and exhaustion. "We've got to decide what we're going to do concerning these curtains."

"Propose the matter be referred back to the next meeting of this committee for a full verbal report by the town hall supervisor, Mr Chairman," said Aubrey Spry quickly.

"Seconded!" roared Edward Hancock.

"It's been proposed and seconded that the matter be referred back," droned Sandra Miles. "All those in favour, please show. Three. Against - two."

The Chairman did not vote this time. She had some sympathy with Clare Newton, there was no doubt about that; the curtains needed to be replaced - or repaired - as a matter of urgency, not left for at least another month. But she was tired of the whole business, fed-up with the trivial bickerings of people who really ought to know better, and partially relieved to see it all put off for another month. At least she'd be able to get home at a reasonable hour.

"The motion is carried," she said wearily. "The matter of the town hall stage curtains will be referred back to next month's meeting of this committee."

She glanced at Paul Hughes sitting to her right. "Are there any other matters, Mr Hughes?"

"None that I'm aware of Mr Chairman."

"Then I declare the meeting closed," she said with an audible sigh of relief. She rapidly picked up her papers, pushed them into the small attache case which she usually carried, bade everybody a brusque 'good night' and speedily left the chamber, most of the committee following closely in her wake.

Edward Hancock and Aubrey Spry were the last to leave, each helping the other on with his coat as they stood just inside the door.

"You know, Aubrey," said Hancock, flicking up the switches and plunging the chamber into darkness, "I can't see us having new curtains in the town hall for a very long time to come."

They passed through the door into the vestibule, and closed the door behind them.

"Why do you say that?"

"Simply because we've got no money to do it. After all, we're talking about a fair bit of money here you know; thousands I reckon, at the end of the day. And we've not got it."

"No, I suppose not. There's no way the Poll Tax can be kept down - as it has been for the past two years - and the council have money for replacing stage curtains as well," replied Spry.

"There was only about four thousand pounds put by for emergencies for the entire year and that was used up months ago when the gang mower had to be replaced - as I recall."

"Exactly," said Edward Hancock, as they went out into the street. "Which means that there'll be no more money until we fix the new charge in May - after the elections."

"We certainly don't want to levy any supplementary charge or spend any of our reserves, before the election," muttered Aubrey Spry. "That'll not look good at all."

"Exactly," said Hancock once again. "Which is why we'll have to make sure no real action is taken on this curtain business until May at the earliest."

"That's no problem, is it? I mean it would probably take until May if we were in a hurry to get the curtains replaced."

Hancock laughed. "Quite so, Aubrey."

They walked to the end of the street, turned the corner and entered the lounge of "The Kings Head" for their customary after-meeting night cap.

------------

# THE BRIDGE

"We come now to 'any urgent business' brought forward at the discretion of the Mayor." said Graham Goodwin, in somewhat melancholy tones. "And I'm sorry to say, it really is urgent. Mr Jefford please."

"Thank you, Mr Mayor," replied the town clerk. "As I informed you right at the beginning of the meeting, Mr Mayor, we have run into considerable problems with the footbridge over the river linking the playing fields with the park. As members might be aware, a safety inspector checks it every four or five years to make sure it's up to standard. Well, he came after lunch today, inspected the bridge - and promptly condemned it."

"What does that mean?" asked Councillor Mrs Edna Shearer.

"It means Mr Mayor, that the bridge will have to be closed to the public," replied the town clerk. "Actually, I'm using the wrong tense, Mr Mayor; it *is* closed to the public. I took it upon myself to instruct the works foreman to get his staff down there this afternoon and block off the entrances to the bridge - and put up signs saying that the bridge is closed from now on. I believe that work's been done, Mr Tynan."

Frank Tynan, the works foreman, nodded wearily from his seat on the other side of the Mayor, then got slowly to his feet. "Yes, it's all closed off now, Mr Mayor," he said in his rather laconic fashion, "but we had a right caper doing it."

"In what way, Mr Tynan?" asked the Mayor.

"Well, we put these big sheets of hardboard each end of the bridge - which blocked off the entrances beautifully. Then we put up the warning signs, and went back to the depot. Well, I don't suppose we'd been back there more than ten minutes when one of our men who'd been down the park trimming a hedge came in to say that vandals had knocked down all the woodwork we'd just put up and heaved it into the river."

"Unbelievable," muttered the Mayor.

"Shocking" snapped Mrs Shearer.

"God knows what the answer is," said Councillor Dennis Drake sadly.

"I blame their parents," grunted Councillor Horace Kirby.

"I'd birch the buggers," rasped Councillor Bill Brown.

"I thought Mr Tynan said the bridge was closed off, Mr Mayor," said Councillor Mrs Clare Dewhurst, getting to the point - as was her custom.

"It is, Mr Mayor," replied Tynan, still without any urgency. "When I heard that the boards had been thrown in the river, I went around immediately to Maxwell's the farm suppliers and bought a roll of this new kind of barbed wire - the stuff that's made of steel so hard that only special wire cutters can slice through it....."

"They'll find some way of cutting it, don't you worry," interjected the cynical Councillor Mervyn Matthews.

"I certainly hope not, Mr Mayor," retorted Frank Tynan. "If the wire was cut away and somebody got onto the bridge, and it collapsed - well, I shudder to think what would happen."

"This council would be sued, that's what would happen," said Clare Dewhurst. "In fact, it could be that we as members of the council could be sued......"

"I fancy that is somewhat unlikely, Mr Mayor," interjected Jim Jefford, the town clerk, urbanely. "There's no way this council - or its members - can be liable as long as we take all reasonable precautions to close the bridge off. And this we have done, of course. Anyway, I don't think the bridge is in any real immediate danger of collapsing even if somebody did walk on it."

"'course it's not going to collapse, Mr Mayor," snorted the veteran Bill Brown. "You could march the household cavalry across that bridge - and their 'orses as well - in perfect safety. Built, that bridge is - built when they knew how to put things together. Over a hundred years old, that bridge. My grandfather helped build it. Craftsman he was. But then, they all were in those days. That bridge, Mr Mayor, will last as long as the Pyramids. How anybody can say it's unsafe is beyond me."

"The inspector gave it a close examination, Mr Mayor, and was in no doubt that the bridge is unsafe," explained Jim Jefford. "Apparently one of the support struts has rusted through and is literally swinging in the breeze."

"Get on, it's been like that for years," rasped Horace Kirby. "But does it matter? I agree with Mr Brown, Mr Mayor - that bridge is sound as a bell. It'll stand for generations, I propose we ignore what the inspector says and keep the bridge open."

"Keep it open, Mr Mayor?" The town clerk sounded aghast. "But we can't keep it open. The inspector has condemned it. The bridge is unsafe - it's as simple as that. If we keep it open we'll be breaking the law, as well as endangering people's lives."

"Endangering people's lives, be damned," snapped Bill Brown. "There's nothing wrong with the blasted bridge, Mr Mayor - as I said just now. I often walk over that bridge when walking the dog, and there's nothing wrong with it at all. I shall continue to take my dog over it."

"I'm afraid Mr Brown won't be able to do that, Mr Mayor," retorted the town clerk, "unless he's willing to crawl through barbed wire."

"Don't reckon I'll have to do that," rasped Brown. "Knowing the hooligans around here that wire's probably been cut through already."

"I hope not, Mr Brown," said the Mayor. "This entire business is costing us enough money as it is without any more vandalism on top. Where the money will come from to take down this bridge and build another, I really don't know."

"Take it down?" spluttered an incredulous Horace Kirby. "Build another? Mr Mayor, with respect I've never heard such nonsense in my life. It'll cost a fortune to knock it down and an even bigger one to put up another."

"Quite so, Mr Kirby," retorted the Mayor. "Unfortunately, though, we've no option. We must have a sound footbridge over the river."

"We have got an option, Mr Mayor," persisted Kirby. "We can repair the old one - simple as that."

"That we cannot do, I'm afraid, Mr Kirby," said the Mayor.

"Quite so, Mr Mayor," agreed the town clerk getting to his feet. "The bridge is beyond repair - according to the inspector. Rust, metal fatigue - you name it, the bridge is suffering from it. We've not had his full written report yet, naturally, but the inspector was most insistent that the bridge be closed down immediately, then demolished. Whether we build another is up to us, of course, but it will cause a few problems to many people in the town if we don't."

"Of course, it will, Mr Mayor," opined Mrs Shearer. "For a start the changing rooms for those using the football, rugby and hockey pitches, and the tennis courts, are on the other side of the bridge in the park. If we've got no bridge it means that they'll have to change then walk to the end of the park, pass over the road bridge, then walk up the main road to the west gate of the playing fields."

"That's not very far," grunted Bill Brown.

"Not very far?" retorted Mrs Shearer in her shrill voice. "Why it's - it's miles. Mr Mayor, the bridge has to be replaced and as quickly as possible."

"I quite agree," snapped Councillor Alan Henson. "The park and the playing fields have been one unit thanks to that bridge for - for over a hundred years. Think of the thousands of people every year who use that area - and use the bridge out of necessity. Of course it has to be replaced - no matter what the cost."

"It's all very well saying that, Mr Mayor," said Dennis Drake in his slow, deliberate way, "but where's the money to come from? It'll cost thousands to demolish the bridge and scores of thousands to re-build it."

"I think we'll probably be able to get a grant towards it, Mr Mayor," opined the town clerk.

"Towards what?" asked Bill Brown sharply. "The knocking down or the re-building?"

"Well - well - well, I'm not totally certain, Mr Mayor," replied Jim Jefford slowly, pulling a handkerchief from his pocket to mop his brow - a habit of his when things were getting a little difficult. "But I'm sure we can get some financial help towards an emergency project such as this."

"Who from, Mr Mayor?" asked the persistent Bill Brown.

"That's a fair question," agreed the Mayor. "Mr Jefford?"

"Well, Mr Mayor, well ..... I feel.......well I'm sure," stuttered the town clerk, "I'm sure there are grants to be had. There are always grants to be had for such work as this - or usually, anyway. Obviously, though, I've not had time to go into it all, Mr Mayor. It was only this afternoon, after all, that the inspector condemned the bridge."

"Yes, that's quite true, Mr Mayor," agreed Councillor Mrs

Daphne Doyle. "It's most unfair to expect answers of this nature at this stage from the town clerk. He must be given some time to find out just what money there is available. With that in mind, I would propose that we defer any decisions on the bridge until our next meeting, by which time Mr Jefford will no doubt have obtained details of assistance we can get towards replacing this bridge."

"I don't object to deferring it for a month, Mr Mayor," said Horace Kirby, "but I'll tell you now, there'll be no money forthcoming from anybody to sort the bridge out. I still reckon we should keep the bridge open; but if the council decides it's got to be closed off, then so be it. But for sure, we'll never be able to afford to replace it, so it's best, in my estimation, just to leave it as it is. We've got the barbed wire across the entrance at each end to stop folk walking across it - and that's all we need do. Far better to spend what little money we do have on something else."

"But Mr Mayor, that's plain silly!" cried Mrs Shearer. "We can't just leave the bridge. Quite apart from anything else, look what an eyesore it would be - a rusting, decaying heap of metal straddling the river."

"Why should it be, Mr Mayor?" rasped Bill Brown. "It's not an eyesore at present, so why should it be later on. Just the opposite I would think; a structure like that built by craftsmen in the age when such people produced only workmanship of the highest quality, should be kept for future generations to see - just like they keep the 'Cutty Sark' and Nelson's flagship. Folk enjoy seeing them, so why shouldn't they want to see our bridge? Why, it could even become a minor tourist attraction."

"With respect to Mr Brown, Mr Mayor - that's plain daft," snorted an exasperated Daphne Doyle. "There's absolutely no point in preserving a bridge which cannot be used."

"Then why do they preserve the Cutty Sark?" snapped Brown. "I've not heard of it carrying any cargoes of tea for some time."

"That's different - obviously different, Mr Mayor," retorted Mrs Doyle. "Mr Brown's being deliberately stupid."

"Nothing deliberate about it in Bill's case," muttered a smirking Alan Henson to his 'neighbour', Mervyn Matthews.

"Who're you calling stupid?" roared Brown. "Mr Mayor, I protest. I've been on this council for over thirty years and nobody's ever insulted me like this before. I demand an apology."

"I'm sure Mrs Doyle meant no offence, Mr Brown," droned the Mayor in as soothing a tone of voice as he could muster. "However, I do feel you should be a little more careful in how you speak of, or to, other members of this council, Mrs Doyle." He gave her a look of gentle reproach as he had said the words of a like nature.

"I didn't mean to offend Mr Brown, or anybody else for that matter, Mr Mayor," retorted Daphne Doyle in her aggressive way. "I was just speaking my mind. What he said was stupid, as I'm sure most members would agree. However...."

"The Victorian Society, Mr Mayor, that's the answer," interjected Edna Shearer excitedly.

"We must apply to them for a grant. They'll pay something towards renovating the bridge, I'm sure."

"Who's the Victorian Society?" asked Clare Dewhurst.

"Well, I don't know that they're called that exactly," retorted Mrs Shearer, "but there is a nationwide society who concentrate their efforts on preserving our heritage - especially things Victorian. I went to a lecture and slide-show about it a couple of years ago, held in the church hall. It was given by - let's see -

yes, it was Mr Jenkins the butcher in Fore Street. Very knowledgeable he was about so many things, and I'm sure he said the society gave out grants to preserve ancient monuments, buildings and suchlike - with Victoriana being very much to the fore. Perhaps Mr Jefford could have a word with him, before the next meeting, about the possibility of getting some money from his society for the bridge."

"You'll have to take a shovel with you," snapped Horace Kirby, directing his words at the town clerk. "He died about twelve months ago."

"Yes - of course he did," agreed Alan Henson. "We used to get our meat there until he died. His shop's an estate agents now."

"Yes, I remember now," chipped in Bill Brown. "Criminal it was, that the planning committee let that go through. Damnit, we've got more estate agents in this town than we've got houses."

"Well, you know what happened there," said Mervyn Matthews, "It's obvious that the committee...."

"I fancy we're straying from the subject, gentlemen," interjected the Mayor. "Mrs Shearer was telling us about this society who give out grants - and that the late Mr Jenkins was connected with it. What we obviously have to do now is to find out if there's anybody else in this town involved with this society or, failing that, the address of the society at county or national level. Perhaps we could leave that to you, Mr Jefford."

"Yes - yes, of course, Mr Mayor," agreed the town clerk with a grimace. How, he asked himself, was he supposed to go about finding out about an organisation which nobody knew the name of and whose only local member, of which anyone was aware, was a dead butcher?

"Waste of time the whole lot of it," snorted Dennis Drake.

"Why do you say that, Mr Drake?" asked the Mayor. "It would seem to me to be a reasonable idea. After all, even if we were to get a grant of just a few hundred pounds out of this society then it would be worthwhile."

"I agree, Mr Mayor - but the fact is that we won't get a grant from them will we?"

"Why not?"

"Simply because such a society will most certainly only be interested in paying out good money if it's going to be used to preserve something Victorian - not to knock it down, Mr Mayor," reasoned Drake.

"That's a fair point, Mr Drake," agreed the Mayor. "I suppose it's impossible to actually renovate the bridge, Mr Jefford?"

"Well, yes, according to the inspector, Mr Mayor. Of course, he only gave me a verbal report. It'll be some weeks, no doubt, before we get the full written report on the matter. He did say, though, that there was no way in which the bridge could be repaired. Its deficiencies are so numerous and widespread that the only realistic course is to take the bridge down - and re-build it."

"And it's impossible to build a Victorian bridge in this day and age," said Dennis Drake.

"Why," asked Mrs Shearer.

"Because if a bridge is built now, it's not Victorian, but a twentieth century one, or, if you like an Elizabeth the Second bridge. It'll be all concrete and girders - like the things they put over motorways. There's not an historical society in the world that'll give a grant towards that, Mr Mayor."

"I see Mr Drake's point, Mr Mayor, but there's no reason why we shouldn't build the bridge in a Victorian style, surely," argued Edna Shearer. "If we were to do that, then it's possible we might be able to get a grant. Besides, it would look nice - in keeping with the character of the town."

"There's no way, Mr Mayor, that any new bridge could be built in the old style," opined Bill Brown, "simply because there's no real craftsmen about these days. I doubt there's a man in this country, let alone this town, who would have the skills needed to work on such a bridge. Skilled men like that passed on years ago. We'll not see their like again."

"Mr Mayor, if I might make a suggestion," said Mervyn Matthews in his softly spoken way.

"Certainly, Mr Matthews." He would be pleased to hear anything sensible which would direct them to some course of action and bring the debate to a close; and if anybody could bring sense to the discussion, then that person was Mervyn Matthews.

"Well, Mr Mayor, it seems to me that the obvious place to look for a grant to help fund the replacement of the bridge is to the district council. I am, of course, as you well know, a member of the district council as well as being on this town council, and generally there are funds put by to help in situations such as we face now. How much there's available, mind you, I don't really know. What with the government cut backs and the added expense faced by the district owing to the subsidence of the swimming pool, I reckon there's not exactly a fortune left. But having said this, there's no reason why we shouldn't have a share of what there is. I'll bring it up at the next meeting of the policy committee - which is on - well - sometime next month. Unfortunately, Mr Sellick and Mrs Bevan, who're also on that committee from the town, aren't here tonight, but I'm sure they'll give full support. So I formally propose, Mr Mayor, that we seek a grant from the district council towards the replacement of the footbridge, and we defer any other action on the bridge until we know whether or not any money is forthcoming."

"Thank you, Mr Matthews," said the Mayor briskly, relieved that they were getting somewhere at last. "Is there a seconder?"

"Seconded, Mr Mayor!" cried Alan Henson.

"Those in favour?" A sea of extended arms swayed in the smoke filled chamber.

"Against?" There was not the slightest movement.

"Carried," droned the Mayor. "Now, there being no further business - or none that I've been informed of at any rate," he added in a tone which brooked no argument, "I declare the meeting closed."

Never a man to linger behind after meetings, Graham Goodwin was out of the chamber almost as soon as his gavel had come to rest on his desk, and was followed, a little more slowly, by the members of the council in ones and twos. Last to leave were Mervyn Matthews and Bill Brown.

"Do you reckon there's any real chance of getting any money from the district for this blasted bridge?" asked the veteran Brown as they passed through the doorway leading from the council chamber.

"Not a hope in hell," retorted Matthews. "To start with the district's got hardly any money what with one thing and another and secondly, as you well know Bill, they wouldn't give the town council a brass farthing even if they had. It'll be a long time before they forgive us for refusing to allow them to park their environmental pollution advisory caravan in the Broad Square car park last Summer. So there'll be nothing coming from them."

"Why did you propose we approach them then?"

"So we could get home tonight. That debate could have meandered on for hours. Graham Goodwin is a good Mayor in many ways, but he's no great shakes in the chair; never knows how to bring a debate to a close."

"But what'll happen when the town's told there's nothing coming from the district?" asked Bill Brown as they stepped out into the street.

"Nothing - that's the whole point, Bill, isn't it?" said Matthews with a shrug of his shoulders. "Let's face it, nothing's going to be done to replace the footbridge - not in the foreseeable future anyway. You and Horace Kirby will get your wish; the bridge will be left there probably until it falls down - and I reckon we'll all be retired from the council, and the world itself, by the time that happens."

"You think that?" Bill Brown sounded somewhat amazed.

"Certainly," replied his companion, urbanely. "After all, where's the money to come from to even take the bridge down, let alone replace it? There'll be nothing coming from the district - though it'll take about five meetings and a like number of months for them to make that a final decision. There'll be nothing coming from any other outside body, will there? After all, there's nobody to apply to as far as I'm aware - certainly such daft suggestions as applying to Victorian Societies, and such like, is a real non-starter. And last, and most importantly of all, the town council haven't got enough spare money to take out one rivet. So that's that."

"We could put up the Poll Tax."

"You're joking, Bill. We put it up last May to help pay for the new windows in the town hall - and there was all hell let loose in the town as you well remember. If we put it up again, I reckon we'll all be tarred, feathered and thrown off the blasted bridge."

Bill Brown laughed. "We could well be tarred and feathered,

Mervyn, but there's no way they'll be able to throw us off the bridge. That's out of bounds - barbed wire both ends.''

Mervyn Matthews smiled in his laconic way, nodded his agreement, and walked slowly towards his car parked further down the street, wishing his elderly companion a gentle 'good night Bill,' as he went.

------------

# THE EMERGENCY COMMITTEE

Donald Nelson had been chairman of the parish council for five years and not once during that time had he ever used a gavel to call a meeting to order. Blessed with a loud and penetrating voice, and, at twenty stones in weight, a considerable presence, a thunderous clearing of the throat and a booming, "let us make a start, ladies and gentlemen, please," or an even louder "quiet, please," when the committee was gripped with excitement, always restored order to the proceedings. So it was on this evening when the "special meeting" was about to commence.

"Let's have a bit of quiet, please, ladies and gentlemen," he rasped. "It's time we made a start. We don't want to be late finishing this evening."

"As far as I'm concerned, Mr Chairman, I don't know why we're starting at all," grumbled Councillor Arthur Hayward. "Why can't this business, whatever it is, be put on the agenda of the normal monthly meeting? There's nothing that urgent, surely?"

"Well, Mr Hayward," replied the chairman. "I'm not really sure myself how urgent the matter is. The point is, though, that the clerk has received a letter from the district council advising us to call a special meeting of this parish council to set up an emergency committee - and it's got to be done before the end of the month. And that, of course, means that our next scheduled meeting would be too late by more than a fortnight. Still, Mr Harvey will explain the situation more fully."

The parish clerk got hastily to his feet, scattering papers like confetti - as was his custom - and immediately launched into an explanation in his fast talking, staccato way. "Thank you, Mr

Chairman," he gabbled. "As you so rightly say, this meeting has been called in accordance with advice given us by the district council. The facts of the matter are these. The district has received instructions from the Home Office that every parish in the district - in fact, every parish in the entire country, for that matter - must form an emergency committee. Of course, our district council won't be responsible for the rest of the country, but merely for the parishes in this district. I only mentioned the rest of the country to show that we in this parish, and in this district, are not being singled out."

"We know that, Mr Chairman," snapped Councillor Peter Parkin. "We're not daft. And we've not got all night either - or, at least, I haven't. I've got a snooker match on at half past eight down the club - and I'm not going to be late for it," he added aggressively. "Please ask the clerk to get to the point."

"I was about to come to the point, Mr Chairman," whined Cyril Harvey in aggrieved tones, "when Mr Parkin interrupted me. However, the facts are these: firstly, as I said just now, every parish and town council throughout the land has to appoint an emergency committee; secondly, it should have not less than six members and not more than ten - and at least half should be members of the council with the others co-opted; thirdly, these committees have to be set up before the end of this month - hence the calling of this special meeting, as I said just now."

"Why?" asked Councillor Mrs Edwina Compton.

"Why what Mr Chairman?" asked the clerk.

"Why does this emergency committee have to be set up before the end of the month?"

"Because it says so in the letter from the district council," retorted Cyril Harvey, the tone of his voice suggesting that he considered he was conversing with an idiot.

"I know it says so in the letter, Mr Chairman - I'm not stupid," rasped Mrs Compton. "What I want to know is why there should be such a rush to set the committee up - and what the committee is supposed to do."

"Well, Mr Chairman, I don't really know why there should be such a rush to set up this committee," replied the clerk. "The letter doesn't give a reason, but ours is not to reason why, as the saying goes. As to what the committee's duties are, I would have thought that was obvious, Mr Chairman. It will be a committee to deal with emergencies."

"What's that supposed to mean?" asked Councillor Alfie Cartwright. "Are we supposed to run around and help the fire brigade fight fires, mop up floods and suchlike? If we are, then I for one don't want to be a member of this committee."

"No - no - no, Mr Chairman, it's nothing like that!" cried a rather exasperated Cyril Harvey. "All emergencies will be taken care of by the fire brigade, police, ambulance service and so on, just as they always have. No, the committee will be there to supervise other kinds of emergencies - or that's as I understand the purpose of it after having spoken to the chief executive of the district council about it. Although, I must admit that he seemed a bit vague about it all himself."

"I was speaking to the chairman of the policy and resources committee of the district council myself yesterday - on another matter," said the Chairman, "but did happen to mention this business about an emergency committee being set up. I naturally asked him what the purpose of it was and he seemed to feel that each parish had to have one to co-ordinate things if the area had drought, floods, that sort of thing; and, of course, a nuclear attack. He and the Chairman of the district council, plus their chief executive, of course, will be the leading organisers of things in the event of such emergencies, but each parish committee will be responsible for the actual running of things in their specific area - or that's how he sees it, anyway." "You might see that lot if there's a drought or a flood about, but you'll not see sight nor sign of them if there's a nuclear attack, Mr Chairman," opined Councillor Larry Parsons, with a grin. "They'll all be in the bunker."

"What bunker's that?" asked Alfie Cartwright.

"What bunker?" Parsons voice was full of incredulity. "I thought everybody knew about the bunker. It's the secret one built underneath Ferndown Hill. You must have heard about it. Derek Allen's Plant Hire - just up the road here - supplied all manner of plant to excavate it; I do know that - he told me. What it is, they've built a nice snug little place there so if a nuclear attack comes, they'll be safe whilst the rest of us are fried."

"I don't think it's quite like that, Mr Parsons," admonished the Chairman, gently. "As I understand it, the bunker is for those leading citizens of the district, responsible for the organising of all emergency and basic services in the district, to be able to go into so that they can continue to maintain some semblance of administration over the area - so that total anarchy will be avoided. It's difficult to see how they can do that if they're locked in a bunker, but that's the basic idea as far as I'm aware. Still, we shouldn't be discussing this - it's secret."

"Secret, Mr Chairman?" snorted Larry Parson. "I reckon the football results of a Saturday afternoon are more secret than this. Oh, yes, I know it's supposed to be secret, but the daftness of that was really shown up when the district council publicly invited tenders from builders to construct a secret bunker. Classic one, that was."

The Chairman smiled. "Yes, that's true enough," he agreed, "but still, I fancy we've spent long enough talking about something which isn't the responsibility or business of this council. The formation of an emergency committee is what we're here to discuss - and set up. Mr Harvey, please."

"Thank you, Mr Chairman. As I see it, we have, tonight, to decide who should be on the emergency committee....."

"Shouldn't we first decide how many we want on it?" interjected Peter Parkin.

"I was about to come to that, Mr Chairman, when Mr Parkin interrupted me," snapped the clerk. "Yes, we have to decide just how many we have on the committee."

"None, Mr Chairman, that's what I'd have on the committee - none," snorted Arthur Hayward.

"This is the biggest load of nonsense I've ever heard in my life. If the bomb falls we'll all be blowed to kingdom come; where floods are concerned, this parish is so high above sea and river level that if we're flooded it's the Judgement come; and when it comes to drought, that's for the Water Board to sort out, not us. I propose we have nothing whatsoever to do with any of it."

"But, Mr Chairman, with due respect, Mr Hayward is talking rubbish!" cried an exasperated parish clerk. "The point is....."

"Hang on mister - nobody speaks about me like that," roared Arthur Hayward, his face the colour of raw liver. "I've been on this council for over twenty years and no councillor has spoken to me like that before, let alone a parish clerk. I demand an apology."

"Damned right, Mr Chairman," snorted Councillor Denzil Colbourne. "We give our time for no reward, except that we know we're serving the people of this parish. We certainly don't do it, though, for the paid servants of this council to insult elected members. The parish clerk should apologise to Mr Hayward immediately."

"Yes - yes, I do agree," said the chairman evenly, hoping to take the sting out of the situation. "However, I'm sure the parish clerk has spoken in haste and frustration. Certainly I'm sure he meant no offence to Mr Hayward - is that not correct Mr Harvey?"

"Yes, indeed, Mr Chairman," replied the clerk hastily. "I most definitely meant no offence to Mr Hayward, and if I've given it then I apologise unreservedly. It was just that I got exasperated when Mr Hayward proposed the one course of action that's not open to us. You see, Mr Chairman, the point is that this is not a directive from the district council. If it were then there might be ways we could take - well, take minimal action on it. The reality, though, is that this instruction only comes through the district council; they're not the authors of it. The Home Office is the power behind this and so we've no option but to do what they instruct. After all, a parish council such as we are cannot fly in the face of the Home Office."

"No, quite, quite, Mr Harvey," agreed the chairman. "Obviously, we have to do what they say. So we must decide as to who's going to be on the committee - and how many, as Mr Parkin said just now. Also, we have to decide who we wish to co-opt onto the committee."

"I reckon we should have the minimum number, Mr Chairman," opined Alfie Cartwright. "The more members of any committee there are, the more yap and the less action."

"Yes, that's true enough, Mr Chairman," agreed Edwina Compton. "Although I wouldn't expect much action from such a committee, no matter how many members it has. Let's face it, we as a council aren't exactly noted for action. I mean, we all sit here and talk about things, around things and from time to time, through things - but we never seem to do anything."

"But we're not here to do things, Mr Chairman," snapped Arthur Hayward. "That's not the purpose of this council - or of any council for that matter. My father was a member of this council for over thirty years and he always said that if you didn't do anything, then you couldn't do anything wrong. And he was right. We're here to keep the Community Charge down - that's our main purpose. And, of course, we're here to listen to the chargepayers complaints. But, having said that, they don't really expect us to do anything about them; just as long as we listen. I've seen these men and women of action over the years; they never last. Either they burn themselves out, or the electors throw them out.

No, I never trust action, Mr Chairman."

"No - no - quite, quite, Mr Hayward," muttered the chairman. "There's much in what you say. However, our purpose at the moment, is to decide just how many members the emergency committee should have. You said just now, Mr Cartwright, that you thought the committee should have the minimum number of members," he continued, looking vaguely in the general direction of Councillor Cartwright. "Was that a proposal?" Alfie Cartwright shrugged his shoulders. "If you like, Mr Chairman," he replied.

"Thank you. Do I have a seconder?"

"Yes - I second that," said Peter Parkin, briskly. "Anything to get this silly meeting over and done with."

"That's hardly the spirit, Mr Chairman," complained Councillor Mrs Audrey Anderson. "I'm sure Mr Parkin would be the first to welcome the efforts of an emergency committee if he were flooded out.''

"If I was flooded out, I reckon I'd welcome the efforts of St Peter," he snorted. "Seeing as I live on possibly the highest spot in this generally very high parish, the day flood waters lap at my door will be the Judgment Day itself."

"Well, you know what I mean," snapped Mrs Anderson. "I believe it's important for us to have an emergency committee. It's rare I agree with the Home Office, but I think they're right - for once."

"If Mrs Anderson's so much in favour of this committee, Mr Chairman, perhaps she ought to serve on it," retorted Peter Parkin. "I certainly don't want to. "

"I would be pleased to serve on such a committee if nominated, Mr Chairman," replied Audrey Anderson.

"It sounds to me like the sort of committee which might actually do something constructive - something to help the chargepayers of the parish when they really need it. I can't think of any other sub-committee of this council that ever really helps anybody at anytime. In fact, I can't think of any other committee which actually ever does anything at all," she concluded, with spirit. Her acerbic remarks failed to provoke a response - largely because the chairman, keen to bring the entire business to some conclusion, quickly came in with a question to the parish clerk.

"It's been proposed and seconded that we have the minimum number possible on the emergency committee," he boomed, even louder than usual. "Perhaps you would tell us how many the minimum number is, Mr Harvey."

"Six, Mr Chairman - as I said a little earlier."

"Six, so that means we appoint three councillors and co-opt

three others from the Parish."

"That's quite correct, Mr Chairman," agreed the clerk in his somewhat pompous way.

"I thought the clerk said earlier, Mr Chairman, that *at least half* the committee should be made up of councillors," argued Arthur Hayward, "not, just half. The way he put it just then, suggests that more than half of the committee can be made up of councillors - is that right?"

The parish clerk cleared his throat, studied the paper in front of him intently, then looked at the chairman. "Well - yes, Mr Chairman, I suppose it does mean that more than half of the committee can be made up of councillors. However, I feel that the spirit of the directive of the Home Office is that there be an equal partnership between the council and the local community. With that in mind, I do feel that it would be fairest if the council have just the three on the committee, with the other three members being co-opted from the community."

"I don't give a damn what the parish clerk feels, Mr Chairman," rasped Hayward. "It's the elected members of this council who make the decision here - not the paid officials. The fact is, if we've got to appoint such a daft committee as this, then for heaven's sake let's keep control of it. Four members of the council, with two co-opted from the parish - that's my proposal. If we have equal numbers, then the co-opted members will be trying to run things; I've been on those sort of committees before - they come up with all sorts of Tomfool ideas and the whole thing becomes a farce. Anyway, it's not democratic for non-elected folk to have too much say. After all, we've got to answer to the voters every four years - so it's only right that we make all the decisions."

"I agree entirely with Mr Hayward, Mr Chairman," said

Peter Parkin, "and I second his proposal."

"Well, I disagree with Mr Hayward," snapped Mrs Anderson. "I would have thought that democracy was all about people having their say and putting forward new ideas. We could certainly do with it on this parish council. I've been on it for two years now, and I've not heard a really positive idea or comment put forward yet on any subject whatsoever.

This is a thoroughly moribund body."

"I object to that, Mr Chairman," stormed Alfie Cartwright, an angry, almost malevolent expression on his face. "There's been no lack of good and positive ideas and proposals put forward to this council by the members over the years. And I'm talking about many years as well - over twenty in my case. I take particular exception to somebody like Mrs Anderson, who's only been on a dog's watch, accusing us of not doing our job - because that's what she's saying in effect. And I object to being called mor- mor- mor ..."

"Moribund," assisted the chairman.

"Yes - exactly," rasped Cartwright, "I object to being called that."

"So do I, Mr Chairman," said Larry Parsons. "There's nothing moribund about this council. Just the opposite in fact; we're always involving ourselves in schemes to help the people of the parish."

"Such as?" questioned Audrey Anderson, somewhat aggressively.

"Well - well - well, there's scores of things, really," stuttered Parsons. "I can't call them all to mind at the moment, of course, but there's been all sorts of things over the years." He didn't like the way this debate was developing. He needed to counter attack quickly, or else the quick witted Mrs Anderson would have him in trouble.

"Still, instead of Mrs Anderson finding fault - unfairly - with the rest of us, perhaps she should make an effort to be constructive herself," bellowed Councillor Parsons, his voice suddenly aggressive with the confidence of having, to his mind, launched a first class counter offensive. Whether his verbal missile would have sunk Councillor Audrey Anderson would never be known, for Donald Nelson, aware that such an acerbic debate could go on for hours and get ever more bitter - and pointless - decided to intervene in order to return it to the rails along which it should be running.

"I'm sure Mrs Anderson, like the rest of us, makes every effort to be constructive, Mr Parsons," he said soothingly, "However, we're straying somewhat from the subject under discussion, which, may I remind you, is the setting up of an emergency committee in this parish. Now, I've had a proposal from Mr Hayward, seconded by Mr Parkin, that the committee consist of six members, four of whom should be serving councillors, the remaining two members being co-opted from amongst the ratepayers of the parish. All those in favour?"

He noted the wavering raised arms, then called, "against?"

Only Audrey Anderson's arm went up and stayed there. Edwina Compton put her hand up to start with, but then thought better of it and settled for the anonymity of abstention.

"The proposal is carried," said the chairman. "Now we have to decide who is going to serve on the committee. Perhaps we could decide on the four council members first."

"May I propose yourself, Mr Chairman," suggested Denzil Colbourne, "and, perhaps, the chairman of the finance committee and of the properties committee - and one other member."

"Yes that sounds fair enough," agreed Arthur Hayward. "That

is, of course, if you and the other two proposed members are willing to serve, Mr Chairman. I second it, on that condition."

Donald Nelson shrugged his shoulders. "Well, I'm willing to serve, Mr Hayward. After all, I can't imagine us having to meet very often. Floods, famines and nuclear attacks aren't exactly regular occurrences locally.

Mr Keegan, the chairman of the properties committee isn't present this evening, unfortunately, but I would imagine he'd be willing to serve on the committee; the chairman of finance, Mr Parsons, is with us, though, so can answer for himself as to whether he's willing to be on the committee. Mr Parsons?"

The chairman of finance grimaced, then nodded slowly. "All right, Mr Chairman, I'll serve on it," he replied slowly. "it's all a total waste of time, of course, but as you said just now, I doubt we'll meet very often. And I assume we are only appointed until the next AGM of the council?"

The chairman looked at the Parish Clerk, who responded with unusual alacrity. "Naturally, Mr Chairman," he said confidently. "This is just a sub-committee of the council like any other, and has to be re-appointed at every Annual General Meeting. Which means, of course, you can change the constitution of the emergency committee entirely then should you wish to. Of course, it could be that you might not want to do so, but if you did then....."

"Yes, thank you, Mr Harvey," interjected the chairman quickly.

The clerk, in this mood, could witter on forever.

"So we're agreed that Mr Keegan, Mr Parsons and myself should make up the emergency committee?"

There were myriad murmurings from about the chamber, from which the chairman assumed that members were, indeed, agreed.

"I would remind you, Mr Chairman," said the clerk sternly,

"that it has been agreed that the committee have four members. You have only appointed three so far."

"Yes - yes, I know; I am well aware of that," retorted Donald Nelson, untruthfully. "I was about to ask for proposals for the last position on the Committee."

"As she's so keen on it, then I propose Mrs Anderson, Mr Chairman - as I suggested a little earlier," said Peter Parkin.

"Mrs Anderson's been proposed. Do I have a seconder?"

"Seconded," grunted Denzil Colbourne.

"Thank you. All in favour - carried," droned the chairman without even glancing at the councillors spread around the chamber before him.

"Well, that would appear to conclude the business of the evening, gentlemen," continued Donald Nelson, enthusiastically, "so I....."

"Mr Chairman, we have two further members to appoint before the meeting can be closed - surely!" cried the Parish Clerk. "We've appointed the four members from the council, so now we've got to decide who we wish to co-opt. Two people, we're looking for."

"Yes - yes, of course, Mr Nelson," muttered the chairman, an expression mingling annoyance and resignation on his face - there were times when meetings were a total pain. "Do I have any proposals as to who should be co-opted onto this committee?"

"How about the vicar?" opined Alfie Cartwright. "If there's a lot of emergency about, a vicar's essential I would think."

"I disagree, Mr Chairman," snorted Edwina Campion. "At such times, we need practical men and women, people of action. With all due respect to the vicar, I don't see him in that role; I very much doubt he'd see himself in that role, come to that.

He'd be useful if we had to bury people, but I would think that the purpose of an emergency committee was to save people, not bury them. No, I can't agree with having the vicar on the committee."

"Frank Donnelly, in charge of the fire brigade - he should be on it, Mr Chairman," said Peter Parkin. "I mean, they *are* the emergency service aren't they? and trained men. It's obvious one of them must be on the committee, and as he's in charge of the local fire-engine, Donnelly's obviously the man."

"Trained men, be damned," stormed Arthur Hayward. "Have you ever seen them in action? Well, I have," he ranted on, without waiting for an answer to his question. "Never forget it as long as I live. We called them out last year when our chimney was on fire; I wish I'd let it burn. They took a quarter of an hour to turn out to start with - and the station's only a quarter mile up the road from our place. And when they arrived they only had three men aboard - and there's about a dozen on the payroll so I'm told. Then another one turned up on a bike a couple of minutes after they arrived. Fine effort that was too; he came hammering down the road, braked too quick outside our house, went flying over the handlebars, and knocked himself out. So, when they should have been putting out our chimney, the fire crew were organising an ambulance to take this fellow to hospital. Shambles it was. And when they did get round to putting out the fire they got more water on our front room carpet than they did onto the flames. And who was in charge of it all? Why Frank Donnelly, of course. The man was worse than useless. Why, if I had my way I'd....."

"Mr Hayward, I must remind you we're in open committee," admonished the chairman. "I really can't allow such comments about a respected member of this community."

"Respected be damned," muttered Hayward, largely to himself. "I'll certainly oppose him being on the committee," he continued, his voice, this time, carrying to the far corners of the chamber.

"How about Mrs Moss, over at Oakways Cottage, Mr Chairman? I think she'd be ideal," stated Audrey Anderson. "She's a very efficient, level-headed woman - and highly practical. Also, as chairperson of the local Women's Institute, she is used to organising events and people, which has to be an important consideration when deciding who we're going to appoint to such a committee as this."

"I reckon we'll have plenty enough trying to organise things, Mr Chairman," snorted Denzil Colbourne. "It's workers we want - doers, not organisers and talkers. Anyway, I know Mrs Moss, typical school teacher - too bossy by half."

"That's grossly unfair, Mr Chairman," stormed Mrs Anderson. "She's a splendid person, dedicated to helping others, and a tireless worker. Mr Colbourne is talking prejudiced nonsense about somebody he scarcely knows."

"I take exception to that, Mr Chairman," retorted Colbourne. "How can Mrs Anderson state who I know or don't know. I've a good knowledge of this parish and the people who live in it - having been born and bred here, and lived here all my life, which is more than can be said for some members of this council. In fact, it's more than can be said for most members of this council. As for Mrs Moss, it will no doubt surprise Mrs Anderson to learn that I served on a parish hall committee with her a few years back - and it was not an enjoyable experience."

"Mr Chairman, I do object to Mr Colbourne's comments," rasped an angry Audrey Anderson. "Surely he's out of order making such spiteful comments about a respected member of this community, at a public meeting like this?"

"You're quite correct, Mrs Anderson," agreed the Chairman. "As I pointed out to Mr Hayward just now, Mr Colbourne, comments of a personal nature should not be made in open council. I do trust we'll hear no more of it - from anybody."

"A doctor's what we need," opined Larry Parsons. "A committee like this dealing with emergencies will definitely need a doctor on it. Old Doctor Strange is the man. He's lived and practise in this parish for nigh on forty years. He'd be an ideal man."

"Get on, he'd never be sober," snorted Arthur Hayward. "You know what he's like - liquored up half his time."

"Mr Hayward, please," remonstrated the chairman. "These personal attacks and criticisms of leading citizens of this parish are intolerable in open council - as I've already said on two occasions. Let us please have a little more dignity, and thought for others, in our discussions."

"There's something in the idea of having a doctor on the committee," agreed Edwina Compton, "but I wouldn't support the nomination of Dr Strange - simply because of his age. I would have thought that somebody much younger was needed for a committee which, by its very nature, will only be called into operation when some disaster has occurred. I would have thought Dr Strange's junior partner, Dr Anthony, would be the ideal man."

"Get on, the fellow knows nothing," snorted Arthur Hayward. "When my missus went down with 'flu a few weeks back he swore blind it was glandular fever. I never heard such nonsense in my life. I...." He stopped abruptly as he saw the chairman's angry eyes upon him, and the gavel raised to hammer him into silence. As Donald Nelson returned the gavel to the desk top before him, Hayward cleared his throat noisily, and contented himself with an innocuous, "he's not got a lot of experience."

"That's true," agreed Peter Parkin. "But even if he had it wouldn't do us a lot of good to ask him to join the committee."

"Why not?" asked the Chairman.

"Because he's left the area, Mr Chairman. Moved out about a week back. I know because I tried to book an appointment with him yesterday, for him to have a look at my back - playing me up again," he added for the benefit of anybody who might have been interested. Nobody was. "He's moved to a big practice in the London area. I always knew a sharp, progressive fellow like him wouldn't stay around here long."

"Why have we not been told of this, Mr Chairman?" asked an aggrieved Edwina Compton.

"Well, I don't think a local doctor has any obligation to tell the council of his intentions, or the direction of his future career," said Donald Nelson as soothingly as he could - upsetting the somewhat volatile Mrs Compton was something to be avoided when the object was to finish a meeting as soon as possible.

"How about Colonel Marquand over at the Grange, Mr Chairman?" suggested Peter Parkin. "An ex-military man of his rank would be ideal for an emergency committee."

"Nonsense," snorted Audrey Anderson, "the man's senile."

"Mrs Anderson," growled the chairman in his best warning tones.

"I'm not being disrespectful, Mr Chairman," opined the persistent lady, "merely factual. The Colonel is very elderly - well into his eighties I should think - and shows all the signs of advanced senile dementia. It's nothing to be ashamed of; it happens to so many people in advanced old age. In fact it can happen to people when they're merely in middle age."

"Several suffering from it on this council if you ask me," said Arthur Hayward in a loud whisper which was heard in the far corners of the chamber.

Audrey Anderson fixed him with a withering glare, then continued in her positive, almost aggressive way.

"All I'm saying, Mr Chairman, is that Colonel Marquand, though undoubtedly a fine servant to the country in his time, is now far too old to render any useful assistance to an emergency committee."

"'Course he's no good on a committee, Mr Chairman," agreed Denzil Colbourne, "I reckon everybody who knows him realises that. As Mrs Anderson says, he's half daft these days, and would be a liability. But I doubt he'd have ever been any use; men like him aren't. All they're good at is giving orders and leaving somebody else to do the work. We've got plenty enough like him about already. Workers are what we want - folk who'll take their coats off and get stuck in."

"I disagree, Mr Chairman," retorted Peter Parkin. "Mr Colbourne makes it sound as if we're looking for people to dig latrines or some such thing. We're not. We're looking for sound, sensible people who can bring qualities of leadership at a time of crisis. With that in mind, Colonel Marquand would be an excellent man to be co-opted onto this committee. After all, he had a long and distinguished war service and, no doubt, came through many crises and dangers whilst leading his troops."

"Stuff and nonsense," rasped Alfie Cartwright. "He never knew any dangers in the War - or at any other time for that matter. He was in the Pay Corps; I know that for a fact because his wife once told me. He's a qualified accountant; she told me that as well. She's dead now, of course, but she was always a friendly, outgoing woman, and I remember she told me all about the Colonel's military career when I talked to her at a fête, or something or other, which he opened - what, it must be twenty years ago now. He wasn't a career soldier, but was called up at the beginning of the War, and because of his financial qualifications, was put in the Pay Corps. How he ever made it to Colonel, God only knows - but he did, and he was demobbed in 1946. Nice enough old boy in his way, of course, but absolutely useless to have on such a committee as is proposed."

"Ladies and gentlemen, we do seem to be getting nowhere at an alarming rate," said the chairman, somewhat testily. This meeting had, in his estimation, promised to be a time wasting bore and was most certainly living up to that promise. "We really must make a decision as to whom exactly we wish to co-opt onto the committee or else we shall be here all night."

"Well, I propose George Maunder, Mr Chairman," said Alfie Cartwright. "As a butcher it's obvious that he knows all about food and feeding people - which, of course, has to be an advantage at a time of emergency. But even more important than that, he's sergeant of the specials in the parish - which makes him a man of authority well used to keeping public order and so on."

"What, George Maunder - keep order?" Arthur Hayward's voice was pregnant with incredulity. "That's news to me, Mr Chairman. Why, it's common knowledge he's to be found in the snug of the 'King's Arms' well after hours almost every night of the week. And another thing is....."

"Mr Hayward!" thundered Donald Nelson. "I've warned you incessantly throughout this meeting about your - your - well, the only word I can use is 'slanderous' remarks about various members of our local community. I remind you once again, that we're in open council so such remarks are just not acceptable. If it happens again, Mr Hayward," - he lent forward menacingly and fixed the sinning Arthur Hayward with a stare which would have curled the hair of a more nervous man - "if it happens again," he repeated, "I shall have no option but to order you from the chamber."

Arthur Hayward had served on this council with Donald Nelson for very many years - and he'd known him for a lot longer than that. They weren't really friends, but, generally speaking, they'd always got on well both inside and outside the chamber, each having a healthy respect for the other. Hayward certainly knew the chairman to be a man of his word. If he threatened banishment from the chamber for further misdemeanour, then he meant it. A portion of humble pie lay before the veteran councillor, and he knew he had no option but to eat it.

"I apologise, Mr Chairman, if I've stepped out of line," he said meekly. "I've certainly not intended to upset you or anybody else, but I am concerned that if we are to appoint people to this committee - though, as I said just now, I think it's a daft committee before it even starts - we appoint the right people. As I say, if I've gone a bit too far then I apologise most sincerely. Still, all I've really done, Mr Chairman, is to use my background personal knowledge of local people in the interests of the parish as a whole. You, yourself, have often said that it's essential for a local councillor to have wide-ranging knowledge of the place and the people he represents. I am merely falling into line with that sound opinion."

A flicker of a smile played around the chairman's lips, before being pushed away to be replaced by the habitual firm, uncompromising set of the jaw. This was Arthur Hayward at his best, and Donald Nelson had enjoyed every word.

"Thank you, Mr Hayward," he said mildly. "I'm sure you'll not go too far along those lines again. Now, where were we? Oh, yes, we'd had a proposal from Mr Cartwright, that George Maunder be asked to join the emergency committee. Do I have a seconder?"

"Much as I deplore Mr Hayward's attack on the reputation of a man not here to defend himself, Mr Chairman," stated Edwina Compton, judiciously, "I do feel there is some relevance in what he has to say. I do know that Mr Maunder's name is often bandied about in the parish for activities not exactly to his credit. Certainly, he has been named in connection with liaisons with - well, two or three ladies in the village - and whilst it could well be that such stories are not entirely true, I do believe it to be common knowledge that they are not entirely without foundation. With that in mind, I feel bound to support Mr Hayward's broad thrust that Mr Maunder is not entirely suitable to be a member of the emergency committee."

"I've never heard such bigoted, narrow-minded, puritanical codswallop in all my life," stormed Alfie Cartwright. "What, for heaven's sake, has this man's private life to do with his being appointed to an emergency committee? What if he does spend half his life chasing the women of the parish; what if he does spend the other half drinking after hours at the pub...."

"Mr Cartwright, please," interjected the Chairman. "You're going along the same road as Mr Hayward; I would remind you we're in open council here."

"With respect, Mr Chairman, all this talk about being in open council is nonsense," retorted the angry councillor. "I mean, even if we went into secret session on this issue, nobody in this chamber at present would have to leave. There are no members of the public present, no press - nobody except elected councillors. So we can say the same things in open council as we'd say if we went in secret session, without hurting a soul."

"Well - well - well, that's not the point, Mr Cartwright," persisted Donald Nelson. "Things have to be done properly, and in accordance with standing orders."

"Get on," snorted Cartwright, "three quarters of this council don't even know what it says in standing orders - myself included."

"Then I must be a member of the single quarter, Mr Cartwright," snapped the chairman, his face flushed with anger, "because I am very well aware of what it says in standing orders concerning all aspects of conducting meetings. That includes the demeanour of members, Mr Cartwright, and the automatic respect they show the chair. Should such respect be lacking, then the chairman has the right to order the offending member - or members - to leave the chamber. And, should it prove necessary, the chairman has the right to call the police and have the member - or members - forcibly ejected."

"Seeing as we've not got a full-time copper ourselves," muttered Larry Parsons to his 'neighbour', Peter Parkin, "We'll have to get George Maunder around to throw Alfie out of the chamber simply for wanting George Maunder to be on the emergency committee. A right classic this one is."

"Do I make myself clear, Mr Cartwright?" asked the chairman, in a tone of voice which did nothing to disguise his very real anger with the erring councillor.

Alfie Cartwright had rarely seen the chairman as angry as this, and decided not to tempt fate any further. "Yes, you make yourself perfectly clear, Mr Chairman," he said as casually as he was able. "I'll not pursue the matter any further, except to ask that you seek a seconder to my proposition that Mr Maunder be asked to join the emergency committee."

"Certainly," replied the Chairman. He cast his eyes about the Chamber. "Do I have a seconder to Mr Cartwright's proposal?"

Not an arm, hand, or even as much as a finger moved into the air to support Alfie Cartwright. Mr Sergeant of Specials might well have been an ideal man to be on the committee, but the proposal that he should be had caused such a furore that members of the council felt that discretion being the better part of valour, less contentious persons than the hapless George Maunder should be appointed.

"There being no seconder, Mr Cartwright, then obviously Mr Maunder's name cannot go forward for the committee," said the chairman evenly, most of his previous anger having evaporated. "Are there any more proposals as to whom should be on this committee? although I doubt there's many left in the parish who've not already been proposed," he added, wearily. "It seems to me....."

"Point of order, Mr Chairman," interjected Larry Parsons.

"Yes, Mr Parsons?"

"Well it seems to me that we, as a full council, shouldn't be appointing co-opted members of a sub-committee at all. I may be wrong, of course, but I seem to remember that a few years back when we had to appoint another committee for some purpose or other - I can't remember what it was now - we left the co-opting of ratepayers from the parish to the sub-committee itself. I would have mentioned this earlier, before we ever got into this debate on who should be on the committee, but it's only just occurred to me. Perhaps the parish clerk can give a ruling on this."

"I'm sure you're right, Mr Parsons," retorted the chairman enthusiastically - and quickly, before Cyril Harvey had a chance to speak. Donald Nelson was only too well aware that the parish clerk would take half an hour of burrowing into papers and making notes, before coming up with an answer - and that reply would be so vague as to be useless. If this interminable, pointless meeting was ever to be brought to a close, then the bull of prevarication had to be taken by the horns.

"I do seem to recall that members of sub-committees have in the past, been responsible for co-opting folk onto those sub-committees," he continued, hastily. "So, with that being established, there's obviously no need for this council to deliberate any longer as to who should be co-opted onto the emergency committee."

"Are you quite sure that's the correct procedure, Mr Chairman?" asked Edwina Campion, a pugnacious expression on her face. "Personally, I'm not at all happy about it. I feel......"

"Quite sure, Mrs Campion," thundered the chairman, a 'don't dare argue with me' expression on his face.

"Very well," retorted the lady, tersely.

"Good - that appears to be settled then. The emergency committee will consist of Mrs Anderson, Mr Parsons, Mr Keegan and myself, with two further members - not councillors - to be co-opted when we have our first meeting. When will that be, Mr Harvey?"

"When will what be, Mr Chairman?"

"The first meeting of the emergency committee, of course."

The clerk could be so obtuse at times, mused an ever increasingly impatient Donald Nelson.

The parish clerk looked surprised. "Well, obviously, when we have our first emergency," he retorted.

"But that's plain daft," snorted Alfie Cartwright.

"The whole thing's plain daft, from start to finish," opined

Arthur Hayward.

"But there's got to be meetings of this committee to set the thing up, co-opt members onto it and so on. It would be totally stupid to wait until there was an emergency before having a meeting. I've never heard such nonsense in my life," continued Cartwright.

"Well, it says nothing in the directive from the district council about holding a preliminary meeting. It just says we should form a committee," stated the clerk, doggedly.

"That's beside the point, Mr Chairman," stormed an ever more angry Councillor Cartwright. "Surely we've enough commonsense on this council to be able to proceed to act without being expressly told to do so by the district council. If we haven't then it seems to me we're all wasting our time here - and everybody else's as well. We must fix a date for an early meeting of the emergency committee, Mr Chairman."

"Yes, yes, I quite agree, Mr Cartwright," said the Chairman nodding vehemently. "However, seeing as Mr Keegan isn't here, may I suggest that this be put on the agenda for our next full council meeting, next month, when hopefully all four of us appointed to the emergency committee will be here and we can therefore settle on a mutually acceptable date. Members agree?"

A series of grunts indicated that members did agree, though Alfie Cartwright looked none too pleased about it all. "I see your point, Mr Chairman," he acknowledged grudgingly, "but I feel that a date should really be fixed this evening. Not that I'm convinced there's any real need for an emergency committee - we've survived quite adequately over the years without one. But if we've got to appoint one then let's do it properly and fix a time for its first meeting, instead of leaving these loose ends - as we always seem to do. After all, it's this seemingly constant lack of action which gives us a bad image in the eyes of the ratepayers. Still, the council's decided not to fix a date until our next full meeting, so naturally I go along with that."

"Thank you, Mr Cartwright," muttered the chairman.

"It's all very well Mr Cartwright going on about taking action now and tying up loose ends and such like, Mr Chairman," rasped Arthur Hayward, "but I've long believed that the worst thing any council can do is to rush into things. 'Look before you leap' as the saying goes."

"Yes, - indeed, thank you Mr Hayward." Donald Nelson glanced quickly at his watch, then glanced around at the gathered councillors before him.

"Well, that would appear to bring the business to a close, ladies and gentlemen," he said briskly. "We've certainly given the subject considerable airing, and I doubt there's anything else can be added at this stage."

Audrey Anderson, however, had other ideas. "I don't wish to prolong the meeting, Mr Chairman," she said, doing just that, "but I do feel the parish clerk should read out to us just what the duties of the emergency committee are. It would be helpful to know now so that we can give it all some thought before we actually meet."

Cyril Harvey looked perplexed. "Well, I should have thought that the duties of an emergency committee would have been obvious, Mr Chairman," he replied. "Such a committee is there to handle emergencies in the parish."

"I know that, Mr Chairman," she snapped. "I'm not stupid. What I want to know is what are the precise duties as laid down in the directive from the district council. I would have thought the parish clerk would have been well aware of what I meant."

Harvey looked even more perplexed. "Duties? In the directive? But there's nothing along those lines in the directive. It simply says that we must form an emergency committee. It doesn't say what that committee should do, Mr Chairman - naturally.''

"What does the parish clerk mean, Mr Chairman? How can it be natural to be told to form a committee and then not be told what the committee is for and what it has to do. I've never heard anything so absurd - so - so - so mind-bendingly stupid, in all my life!'' roared Councillor Mrs Anderson, her face now almost purple with combined rage and frustration. The parish clerk took no notice of Mrs Anderson's outburst - he'd seen her like this before. In fact he'd seen most members of the council - and numerous previous ones over the years - in similar rages. He merely shook his head sadly, shrugged his shoulders, glanced at the chairman and delivered a verdict half a lifetime in the making.

"There's nothing stupid about it, Mr Chairman,'' he said simply. "It's the way we do things in this country, isn't it? I mean it's one thing for the Home Office, through the district council, to tell us to form a committee, but it's a very different thing for them to try to tell us what we should discuss on it - and what we should do. That, after all, is up to us. That's what we're all here for; that, Mr Chairman, is grass root democracy.''

## THE END